C000142420

COLD REVENGE

by

Bip Wetherell

Copyright 2019 Bip Wetherell

All rights reserved.

The right of the author to be identified as the author
of this work has been asserted by him.

This is a work of fiction. Names, characters, places,
incidents, and dialogues are the products of the
author's imagination or are used fictitiously.

Where locations are used, all characters described
herein are fictitious. Any resemblance to actual
people, living or dead, events or locales is entirely
coincidental.

3

The Gambling Man

Maxwell Horatio Cameron stood 6' 2". His deep brown hair was normally spiked and gelled in the modern fashion but not today.

His hair sported an expensive cut from top London hairdresser Paul Williams. His Armani two-piece black suit, Kurt Muller shoes, and white starched shirt were immaculate. The only true hint of opulence was the Versace black and white-striped silk tie which nestled below the shirt collar tied in a sharp Windsor knot.

Maxwell, 'Maxey' to his mates, was always 'The Man' but today he was 'The Main Man.' He just received his First Class Honours degree from Lincoln University and, as President of the Student Faculty, was about to address five hundred fellow students with approximately one thousand proud parents in the awesome setting of Lincoln Cathedral. All the students had rented their gowns and caps for the ceremony, except Max. He had his made to measure.

Max spent most of the previous evening preparing his speech. He had focused on the achievements of his fellow students, how they would go on to be the future of our great United Kingdom. They would become doctors, accountants and solicitors and secure their own standing in the communities that would welcome them.

Max smiled when he thought of the work they must have put into getting their degrees. He himself had done very little. He had chosen Arts and Media and used his talent for delegation to build a team around him that would go on to produce three film projects, the latest being short-listed for a Channel 4 television award. Max provided the ideas, the rest of the team did all the work, and they all received First Class Honours degrees. Job done!

When Max walked onto to the stage and approached the podium, he decided, at the last minute, to change his mind about the subject of his speech. He originally intended to praise the parents who were attending the ceremony, congratulating them for their hard work and sacrifice in bringing up their children to be the country's future. Instead, he praised his team.

"Ladies and gentleman, I would like to thank my right-hand man, Troy Dickinson, who after helping me visit most of the nightclubs in London, is leaving to work in his father's accountancy practice. I also give my special thanks to a beautiful young lady Pricilla Templeton who accompanied Troy and me on our evenings of entertainment. She is going to join her mother's company selling cosmetics online. Last, but not least, the party animal of the group, William Darling, who is going into partnership with his elder brother selling double glazing.

The audience just sat spellbound. Max could feel the anger of the teachers sat behind him.

He ended his short speech by exclaiming, "I too will follow my father into his chosen profession. Yes, ladies and gentlemen, I leave today to become a full-time professional gambler." He left the stage to complete silence.

The reason Max changed his mind about the content of his speech was because he knew his parents had not made any sacrifices whatsoever, especially his father.

After the degree ceremony, everyone was mingling outside the Cathedral, drinking champagne and taking selfies. Friends were hugging, hats were being thrown in the air. Everyone's parents were looking on proudly, except for Max. He knew there was no point in looking for his father as he was serving eighteen months in Kelmarsh Prison for fraud. Up until his shock announcement about his father's true profession, all of his mates thought Max's dad was a high ranking Royal Navy officer away sailing the seven seas.

As Max pretended to hug his mother, he had to turn away as the aroma of the champagne she was already drinking was mixed with the fumes of last night's vodkas.

"I spoke to your Dad today, he wished you luck." Max ignored her.

"He reckons he'll be out on parole next week."

"The bookies will be pleased," replied Max.

Later that evening, Max sat alone in his study not wishing to go out and party. He opened a very expensive bottle of Glenfiddich whisky, poured himself a large measure and thought back to the first time he realised that he too was to become a gambler.

The pub where he worked part-time to help boost his student loan was having a day out at Towcester Races. They were going there as the landlord of the pub, big Smiffy, had a share in a horse called 'Nags Head' named after the pub. Everyone was going to put a bet on the horse and they were convinced they were onto a sure thing.

So was Max until he wandered over to the ring to watch the horses being paraded. 'Big Smiffy' had given the staff a fifty quid bonus and coupled with one hundred and fifty pounds from his student loan, Max was feeling quite wealthy. He was determined to keep his money in his pocket and not waste any on a stupid bet.

It was then that a horse called 'Toy Flag' caught his eye. There was just something about him. He looked at the card. 'Band Aid' was the short-priced favourite at 2-1, Smiffy's horse was 12-1, and 'Toy Flag' was priced at 50-1. He noticed from reading the race card that 'Toy Flag' had travelled all the way from North Yorkshire down to this Northamptonshire racecourse to jump twelve fences over a three mile trip. The horse looked fresh and alert and was straining at his bit. The handler was struggling to lead him round and when the jockey mounted, the horse reared up on his two hind legs and nearly threw him.

To this day, Max never knew why he went over to the bookies and placed two hundred pounds on 'Toy Flag' to win at 50-1. The bookmaker looked at him as though he was crazy.

Max took the betting slip from the bookmaker and wandered down to the rails to watch the race. His horse was number eight and the jockey was easy to follow with yellow-striped racing colours on a white background making him stand out.

At the end of the first circuit, of the eight starters, three had already fallen with one horse pulled up. 'Toy Flag' was last of the remaining four riders, but Max was convinced his horse would win.

Coming around the final bend, 'Band Aid' and 'Nags Head' were neck and neck. 'Smiffy' and the rest of the staff were going mad. 'Toy Flag' was third.

The two leading horses jumped the last fence neck and neck. There is a long uphill run in at Towcester racecourse so there was still a quarter of a mile to go. 'Toy Flag' met the last fence perfectly and, with a giant leap, gained a few yards on the leaders. All three jockeys were now out of their saddles, one hand on the reins with the other hand whipping their charges to a frenzy.

'Toy Flag' was closing fast but it seemed for a moment it was too late. Max was standing on the rails next to the finish line and he could see the look in the eyes of his horse as all three horses crossed the line together. The steward called for a photograph to determine the winner but Max walked backed to the bookmaker convinced his horse had made the final effort.

The announcement came over the P.A. The winner was 'Toy Flag' at 50-1, second 'Band Aid' at 2-1 and finishing third 'Nags Head' at 8-1.

Max held out his hand as the bookmaker not only handed him his two hundred pound stake back, counting out four individual fifty pound notes, but added another wedge of fifty pound notes, with a bank wrapper around it, stating it held ten thousand pounds. Max won ten thousand pounds plus his two hundred pound stake! He knew then he would never work again. He would not need to get a job.

Max used his winnings wisely. Ten thousand two hundred pounds was a lot of money to an unemployed student. His mother agreed to let Max use her home as security so he could put his winnings as a deposit on a buy-to-let mortgage to buy the student house he lived in. His landlord was retiring so Max was able to negotiate a good deal. The rent the other students paid him more than covered his mortgage payments and gave him an income besides.

His new business was going well and already he was negotiating to buy his third buy-to-let property. There were always students from the university looking for accommodation in Lincoln. Max's mother was pleased at his progress with his property dealings and was telling all her 'coffee morning' friends about Max's new career. When his mother visited him, she was impressed to see Max was driving a white Range Rover Sports and was quick to point out to Max that his father drove a Ford Mondeo. Max was not interested in any of his father's activities until one day his mother mentioned that Max's father was doing rather well in the casinos down in London.

"He'll just lose all the money again, Mum. You never win against the big boys," replied Max.

After his Mother left, Max started to think. He had tried his luck again at a couple of racecourses but he had not experienced 'the feeling' since that day at Towcester. He wondered if his luck would hold in something different from horseracing so he went to London the next day to try his luck but was disappointed as his casino membership application form at the Plaza Casino in the West End had to be checked and it took twenty-four hours to do this.

Max booked into a hotel, did all the usual touristy things the following day, and arrived promptly at six o'clock in the evening as the casino opened. The room was fantastic. The carpet seemed like it was six inches thick, the soft furnishings and curtains were expensive-looking and the waitresses, croupiers and restaurant staff were all female and stunning. The only males were the pit bosses who were there to watch what was going on and to ensure everything was fair and above board.

The casino soon filled up with all nationalities coming to spend an evening gambling. Max sat at the bar drinking sparkling water as he wanted a clear mind if he was to risk his hard-earned cash.

He walked about and soon discovered the roulette wheel. 38-1 odds were just too much to risk. He noticed there were several private rooms for high-roller poker players. Too rich for Max's blood now, perhaps in the future.

The game he settled for was Blackjack, 21 or Pontoon or, in France, 'Vingt et Un'. He felt it was the only game he could influence by counting the cards and getting a feeling what card was going to be dealt next. All the other games were just games of pure chance.

Max chose the table with the most beautiful dealer and noticed, on her name tag, that she was called Lana. Max sat in the seat furthest away from the dealer and put one hundred pounds on the table. The reason was he wanted to watch how the other four players fared until it was his turn. Perhaps he could get 'the feeling' after watching what everyone else was doing.

Lana changed Max's one hundred pounds for gambling chips and Max left twenty pounds worth there for his first bet. He looked around the crowed room and started to really enjoy the atmosphere. He noticed the maximum bet was five hundred pounds but he thought he would start small until he felt comfortable in what he was doing. Max tried a couple of times to catch Lana's eye so he could give her a smile but croupiers were under strict instructions not to communicate with the customers. The stern-faced pit bosses, sitting behind the croupiers, were there to make sure this did not happen. Max played for a couple of hours and decided to call it a night and left the casino a couple of hundred pounds up and went back to his hotel. He hadn't had any sort of 'feeling' but decided to stay another day and try his luck the following night.

Once again, he went to Lana's table the next evening and had a cracking night. The 'feeling' had returned! He bet high when he had 'the feeling' and bet low when 'the feeling' wasn't strong. He made just over £1000. Not bad for a night's work!

He decided to call it a night but was pleasantly surprised when Lana came across to the cashier's desk and congratulated him on his winnings. "I work for the owners of this casino, Ladbrokes Gambling, and I was wondering if you would be interested in entering the annual Ladbrokes Gambling competition which is being held in Spain?"

Max asked her to repeat what she had just said pretending he was a bit deaf. The truth was he just wanted her to speak again and not leave. Max thought to himself if it meant he would see Lana again, he would definitely enter the competition.

"Will you be working at the event?" asked Max.

"Yes," replied Lana, 'not only do I work on the night but I help promote it. There are entries from all over Europe." Lana then asked if Max was related to a Richard Cameron as it was an unusual name. Max nodded and said Richard was his father.

Lana went on to say that Richard had entered the competition and wouldn't it be nice if they could meet up in Spain. Max decided not to tell her that would be the last thing he would want to happen. Lana said goodnight and that she hoped to see him in La Manga.

The next day, Max sent off the £500 entrance fee and was pleased when he received a call from a rather nice lady to say he had been accepted and she asked him for his e-mail details so she could send the itinerary direct to him.

Max excitedly awaited the day when he would fly to the venue, La Manga Resort in Spain, and try his luck at winning £10,000 and a trip to Las Vegas where he would play in the World Finals and, more importantly, have a chance to see Lana again.

***

La Manga Club in Spain was fantastic. Ever since he landed at Murcia International Airport, everything had been five-star for Max. Ladbrokes Gambling had pulled out all the stops. From the limo to the hotel, to his premier suite overlooking the golf courses and the Mediterranean, to the fabulous five-course a la carte meal in the superb Ampola restaurant, Max had been treated like a celebrity. The only blot on the landscape was, at dinner, he had not managed to sit next to Lana.

He had been invited to dine with the staff of Ladbrokes so he happily declined room service.

Instead of grabbing a couple of hours sleep before the competition began in the Casino, he thought he would use the opportunity of dinner to grab the chance to consolidate that first meeting with Lana and to see if that feeling of excitement was still there between them, or had he imagined it.

Unfortunately, Lana was seated at the far end of the dining table so Max never got the chance to speak to her.

After dinner, he went back to his room to change. He had bought a new Savile Row dinner jacket for the occasion and after a shower and a shave, he got dressed. He looked in the mirror to confirm that everything was perfect and went to the lift to make his way to the basement of the hotel where the casino was situated. Two personality girls from Ladbrokes were at reception in the casino to meet and greet the contestants and one of the girls showed him to the second blackjack table in the room. He was pleased to see Lana was his croupier. Also, he was sitting in his preferred seat, number five.

Had Lana organised this? He hoped so.

The first table already had five contestants sitting including his father, who Max gave a curt nod to. He had been told earlier by the manager of Ladbrokes Gambling that his father had qualified for the La Manga tournament and the manager was surprised at Max's negative reaction to the news. Surprisingly, the second table where Max was due to sit had an old, rather large, lady waiting. Max turned to his hostess to enquire who the lady was and was surprised to hear the lady had won the competition the previous year.

There were five tables to accommodate the twenty-five regional winners from all over Europe. The casino was filling up with the spectators who were waiting to watch the action and you could already feel the atmosphere building up.

"Ladies and gentleman, on behalf of Ladbrokes Gambling, welcome to the 2020 Blackjack European Competition to decide who wins the ten thousand euro first prize along with automatic entry to the World Final in Las Vegas later this year. The rules are simple. The first player to win ten thousand euros will be the winner. Each player is allowed only one thousand euros as a stake and the minimum bets are one hundred euros and the maximum bets are five hundred euros. If no one manages to win tonight, the competition will be declared null and void with no trip to Las Vegas. So, as you see ladies and gentlemen, unless you plan your strategy carefully, it could be an early night for you." The crowd laughed at this.

"Before we begin, each player has been allocated their seat by their own courier. This was done randomly to ensure fairness for all contestants. Everyone, please welcome the croupiers and the pit bosses into the room and let the competition begin." There was an enthusiastic round of applause as the croupiers took the their seats with the pit bosses sitting behind them to ensure fair play.

A hush descended on the room as the contestants moved into their allocated seats. Max was pleased with his fifth seat as he would be the last to be dealt the cards from the croupier. He felt he could get a feel for what was going on after watching the other four players play. He was really pleased to see Lana looking as beautiful as ever. He looked across but failed to catch her eye.

All five players had one thousand euros of chips and after everyone had placed their initial bets, Lana, having done a lengthy shuffle, dealt the cards from a three-pack shoe. Max was amazed that player number two had already bet the maximum bet of five hundred euros. Max's strategy was to start slowly and wait to see if the 'feeling' came along. He bet the minimum of one hundred euros. The old lady next to him bet two hundred. *Fortune favours the brave,* thought Max. *Let's just wait and see.* Everyone, including Lana, was dealt a face card apart from Max. He was dealt a two of hearts. Lana covered everyone's bets. The guy next to Max could win one thousand euros on his first hand!

Lana dealt the second cards. Max received an ace. One or eleven points, depending on what number you need. He needed twenty-one to win. The other three players were all dealt high cards and they decided to 'stay' and not accept the offer from Lana for another card.

Max tapped the table to indicate Lana should deal him another card. She dealt him a ten. *Brilliant,* thought Max, *twenty-one.* His joy was cut short

17

when Lana dealt herself an ace. "Vingt et un," he said. Twenty-one. An unbeatable hand when you have an ace and a ten to make up your hand. Lana scooped everyone's chips into her tray and dealt everyone another card saying "Place your bets please!" The whole thing had lasted less than a minute. The casino made several hundred euros in less than sixty seconds and Max and the other players were nowhere near winning the first prize. You could see why casinos always came out on top. The game carried on with Max winning some hands but losing as many.

The guy second in from the dealer, the one who was betting the maximum in every game, soon lost all his money and, grumpily, made his way to the bar.

Max asked for a toilet break. He was hoping when he came back, his luck would change. The lady next to him was playing well and it looked as though she was on the way to winning yet another competition. The one thing that did cheer Max up was, on his way back from the toilet, he noticed his father's chair on the first table was empty. Max was pleased his Dad had lost. *His dad was a born loser,* thought Max.

When he sat, Lana opened up another fresh set of cards, shuffled the three packs comprehensively and inserted one hundred and fifty-six cards into the shoe. Before she dealt, she looked over at Max. *Was that a hint of a smile he had seen?* "Place your bets please," said Lana. Everything changed for Max. He had 'the feeling' again. He counted the cards and knew when he was being dealt a high card or a low one and he would bet accordingly.

A few hours later, Max glanced at the pile of chips next to him belonging to the large lady. She had started losing. Max's pile was getting bigger and bigger. The atmosphere in the casino was electric. Max looked around. There was only him and the large lady left still playing. The other three tables were empty of gamblers.

Customers and fellow players formed a circle around his table to watch the action and gasped when Max not only bet the maximum on his place, he also bet five hundred euros on the empty places. A two thousand euro gamble.

Lana dealt place one a Jack of Spades, place two a Ten of Clubs, place three the Queen of Clubs, the lady a Four of Hearts and Max, wait for it, an Ace. Lana hesitated as she dealt herself her first card. She turned it over. Lana dealt herself an ace as well, drawing yet another sharp in-take of breath from the audience. Is this make or break for Max? Is he going to lose all of his four five hundred euro bets?

Lana dealt the second cards. The first four places, including the large lady, were dealt a face card. The audience went crazy when Lana dealt Max the Jack of Spades. 'Vingt et un', twenty-one! It now all depended on what card Lana would deal herself. If she dealt a face it would be a draw between her and Max and the other four spaces would lose their stake. No-one would win the bet. Max would keep one five hundred euro bet but lose the other three.

Lana looked up at the crowd who were all looking at her expectantly. You could hear a pin drop. Lana dealt herself a card and slowly turned it over. It was a two. The crowd erupted. Not only had Max won the bet between him and Lana but 'Vingt et un' paid out one and a half times the original bet, giving Max twelve hundred and fifty euros. Now Lana had to play the empty places plus the large lady. Places one, two, and three all stayed on twenty. The large lady, on fourteen, called for a card. The Seven of Hearts. Unbelievable! Twenty-one, she had won.

Lana placed another one hundred euros on top of the original one hundred euro stake. The large lady was pleased. But what about the other three places? A total of fifteen hundred euros staked with Lana holding two cards worth twelve points and the other three all holding twenty points. Lana needed a nine to win with twenty-one points. She looked up at the crowd again. She cast a glance behind her at the Pit Boss who was watching everything carefully.

She flipped her third card over. It was a King. Twenty-two points! Too many! The crowd roared. Max had won all four bets. The first three places had doubled their stake to one thousand euros each. This, coupled with Max's 'Vingt et Un' winnings of twelve hundred and fifty euros, meant he won four thousand, two hundred and fifty euros in one hand. Max had already won six thousand seven hundred and fifty euros so in total he had won ten thousand euros. He had won the competition. He was going to keep all of his winnings and he was going to Las Vegas. Fantastic!

The director of Ladbrokes Gambling presented Max with a bottle of champagne after he had cashed in his chips. "Ladies and gentleman," the director announced over the house P.A. system, "can I present to you the 2020 winner of the trip to the final in Las Vegas, Mr. Max Cameron."

Everyone wanted to buy Max a drink to help him celebrate his winnings, but Max feigned tiredness as there was only one place he wanted to be. He got Lana's room number earlier on from the concierge of the hotel and, as he made his way in the lift to the top floor of the hotel, he couldn't help but smile to himself. He had the champagne, he had the prize money of ten thousand euros in brand new 100 euro notes, plus his original one thousand euro stake money. All he had to do now was to get the girl.

Champagne in hand, he stood at Lana's door to the room and knocked gently. He could hear someone approaching and Max saw the handle turning. It was Max's dad! Max's jaw dropped! The site of Lana lying on the bed in a flimsy nightie didn't help.

"How can I help you, Son?" Max's father was smiling as he spoke. Max just handed his father the champagne and walked away.

Well, as they say, "You can't win them all!"

Can a Worm Truly Turn?

Phil Jones was a genius, an electronics genius to be precise. After helping the creation of the first Apple Mac computer, he had been offered a job in their new product department and, more importantly, he had been given Apple shares which, at the time amounted to ten thousand dollars but were now worth millions. He was also, unfortunately, the world's biggest hen-pecked husband.

Mrs Olivia Jones was a complete and utter bitch. She had met Phil a couple of years ago, at a computer convention where she was working as a 'personality girl' doing the 'meeting and greeting' giving you a broad welcoming smile and a choice of champagne or orange juice.

Olivia had no interest in Phil the Nerd (as she now refers to him) until she heard his speech how he had developed Apple's latest gadget, the iPhone, and how lucky they all were as their shares in the company would make them all billionaires.

At the sound of the word 'billionaire,' Olivia sucked in her already slim waist, stuck out her already ample chest and made her way to the Ladies to powder her nose. She had to look her best if she was to capture the rich husband that had always been part of her life plan.

Now two years on, she was living the life. She bought herself a small part in an up-and-coming Bruce Willis movie and could now tell her friends she was going to be, at last, the movie star she had always dreamed of.

The only difference between their Los Angeles mansion and that of their neighbours, apart from the fact that theirs had an indoor pool and an outdoor pool, was they had no servants. The staff quarters were empty. The two Rolls-Royces and the Mercedes sports car in the triple garage had no chauffeur to drive them. The $100,000 kitchen had no chef to work in and there was no housekeeper to manage the staff. So how was it that number 2 Hollywood Drive was always immaculate, the pools were always sparkling clean and always at the right temperature, and the cars were always brightly polished? It was because Phil did all the work and I mean, all the work.

He prided himself in the fact that he could turn his hand to anything. With the aid of the internet and a couple of lessons from Gordon Ramsey, Phil was now a recognised gourmet chef. It took him only a matter of days to work out the manuals of both Rolls-Royces and the Mercedes. The engineering behind maintaining both pools was child's play and with only two people living in the house, it was a matter just a couple of hours a day to keep it spotless.

Phil worshipped Olivia. How he had managed to marry such a beautiful woman, he would never know. Well, after all, didn't Marilyn Monroe marry Arthur Miller. Some women obviously preferred the more mature man and Phil always looked forward to the kiss on the cheek that Olivia offered up every morning when he brought up her breakfast tray always complete with a red rose.

Having separate bedrooms didn't bother Phil as it gave him a chance to spend what little time he was allowed to develop his new idea for Apple, the iPhone hologram. His dream was to create a holograph of the person you were facetiming so not only would you be able to see them, they would be in the same room as you.

Phil got used to the shrill cry of 'Philippppp' every time Olivia needed anything and the to-do list on the kitchen fridge was kept full by Olivia so Phil always had plenty to do. Phil made no sexual demands on his wife as, although she had promised to love, honour, and obey him at the Church on their wedding day, she declared that things were a bit delicate down there and "wouldn't just staring at her tits be enough!"

Strangely enough, it was enough! Olivia had a superb body which he occasionally got a glimpse of when he was making her bed and she would waltz naked into the room from the shower and scream at him to "get out at once." Occasionally, as a treat, Olivia would swim naked in the pool and it gave her a perverse pleasure to call out to Phillip to bring her a cocktail. Philips hand would be shaking as he passed the glass over to her whilst she was laying naked on the sunbed.

All in all, Phil thought they were happy. He didn't mind doing all the work because he did like everything to be immaculate. His laundry skills were second to none. On his occasional trip away from the house, usually to get Olivia even more cash from the bank, he prided himself on his silk shirts and trousers that had been ironed so well you would cut your finger on the creases.

Olivia was always busy. Every day, she had lunch with friends. Most evenings, there were production meetings about the new movie. Olivia was now attending expensive acting lessons as her part had been increased from one line to a small dialogue and she wanted to get it just right as, obviously, after the film's release, she was bound to be offered more parts.

Thinking back, Phil thought his life completely changed the day one of the film producers came to the house. It was very unusual to have visitors, so Phil was caught unawares when the doorbell rang and he answered after completely forgetting to take his pinny off and remove the duster from his hand.

Naturally, the visitor thought he was some kind of butler and marched into the library, announcing he had a meeting with 'Miss Olivia deGrande' and would he kindly inform the lady of the house that Matt Dawson, from MGM Pictures, was here for their one o'clock appointment to go through the scenes from the up-and-coming movie.

Like the idiot he was, Phil was only too pleased for Olivia as this meant her part was even bigger than she hoped. Olivia came down the grand stairs looking stunning, a low-cut full-flowing dress outlining her superb attributes. She thrust a list of items at Phil which she required from various boutiques and told Phil he could take the Rolls but not to be back before 5pm as she and Mr. Dawson had work to do and, under no circumstances, were they to be disturbed.

When Phil returned from his errands, Olivia was sitting watching her favourite soaps on the TV. There was no sign of the visitor. Things went back to normal when Phil went into the kitchen to prepare dinner and heard Olivia screech the words "Coffee - Now!" As usual, Phil obeyed just like a puppy dog.

He thought no more of the visitor until he took Olivia's breakfast up the following morning. Two things disturbed him. The first thing was there was no kiss offered up and secondly, the other side of the king-sized bed had been remade by someone rather than himself. No nurse in any hospital could make a bed as immaculate as Phil. He couldn't have imagined Olivia doing such a menial task. Has Matt Dawson been in his wife's bed? Desperately trying to give his wife the benefit of the doubt, Phil thought perhaps they were rehearsing a bedroom scene for the new movie.

Later that night, Phil decided on a plan of action that would bring him nearer to the truth of his wife's comings and goings and remove all doubts about her being unfaithful. He silently entered Olivia's bedroom and retrieved her iPhone which was always plugged in beside her bed. He went back into his room and switched on his computer.

Over the last couple of years, Apple had been working secretly with the U.S. Army to develop software for the iPhone. The first military 'Find a Friend' iPhone meant that every General knew the exact position of every soldier under his command on or off the battlefield. The camera in the military model had a full 360 degrees specification so the soldier could have all-round vision. Phil had also developed an App for the iPhone that, apart from fingerprint recognition to switch it on, the phone had eyeball recognition before it would operate and when it was in the 'off' position, the phone radiated a very strong magnetic field so the phone would be held against anything made of steel, usually the soldiers belt, ensuring the phone was never lost.

These were the apps that Phil worked through the night to place in his wife's phone. Not only would he be able to see who his wife was with, he would be able to record their voices and actions. The final application to be installed was one he had been working on but hadn't yet been field tested. It would be interesting to see how effective it would be.

The next day, Olivia took the Mercedes to downtown Hollywood to have lunch with her 'Personality Girl' friends, all of whom were struggling to find modelling work but had bodies that would ensure regular work serving tables at Hooters. Phil watched events on his computer and listened to endless tales of gossip concerning this movie star screwing yet another movie star.

One of the girls asked 'How's Phil doing?' Olivia replied, 'Phil, the nerd, is doing as he's told.'

Phil turned off the computer so he didn't have to listen to the women laughing at him.

Phil listened in a couple of more times during the week but heard and saw nothing of interest.

It was when Olivia announced she was away on business that weekend that Phil's heartbeat quickened. He didn't even ask her where she was going determined to keep up his lap dog image so as not to arouse any suspicions.

After his dinner on the Friday night, he tuned into Olivia's phone to find out where she was. Wherever she had decided to go, for the first time ever, she hadn't taken her phone with her! Using the 360 app, Phil determined the phone was on a bedside cabinet obviously in a hotel somewhere. The picture was high quality and the sound even picked up the ticking of the bedside alarm clock. Now it was just a matter of being patient.

Four hours later, there was the sound of giggling and doors being opened. Phil turned on the video feed. Olivia and Matt were passionately kissing, grabbing at each other's clothes, both desperate to be naked. Their moans of passion could be heard clearly from Phil's computer. Matt turned Olivia around and bent her over the bed. Her contorted face filled the screen of Phil's computer. Phil could only look at the tits that he was never allowed to touch bouncing up and down to the banging movement from the rear of his wife's naked body. It was then that he turned the magnetic app on.

The phone leapt from the side of the bed onto Olivia's right ear attracted by the metal of the dangling earring. Olivia grabbed at the phone and tried to remove it from the side of her face. For all intents and purposes, it looked as though she was making a call whilst having sex. It was stuck fast, impossible to be moved. Now was the time for the experimental app to be used.

It only took a few seconds for Olivia to realise the phone was getting warmer. She called out to Max but he was too far down the road to stop now. When he finally came, he fell onto the bed and went to hold Olivia who was still trying to remove the phone from her right ear. It was getting hotter and hotter. She started to scream, "Get this off my ear. It's burning me."

Matt tried to remove it but only succeeded in burning his hand. It was then, at a distance of 22.2 miles away, that Phil turned the app to full. The magnesium inlay in the phone exploded.

The smell of burning flesh mingled with the terrifying screams of the naked Olivia. Matt picked up the house phone and demanded that they send an ambulance straight away. Olivia's screams turned into heavy sobs until she became unconscious with a burning iPhone buried into the side of her head.

Phil looked on dispassionately. There was nothing quite like watching your wife having sex with another man to take all the love you felt completely out of the relationship. He was actually chuffed his latest military app had worked. The full model was going to be designed to blow the target's head off, not just burn them. All they needed to do was sell these 'cheap' iPhones to bodyguards surrounding the top terrorists of this world and the results would be better than the existing drone set up. The boys in Washington will be pleased.

Talking about the boys from Washington, it took Phil a couple of hours going through his statement that his wife had somehow picked up one of his military iPhones by mistake that caused this dreadful 'accident'.

Phil visited Olivia every day in hospital. He took her flowers and when he kissed her cheek, he made sure it wasn't the heavily scarred one. The plastic surgeon had done a brilliant job, but let's just say there would be no more 'Olivia deGrande'.

On the day he took her home from hospital, he sat her down in front of the TV, made her a coffee, then came back into the room, passed her coffee and sat down opposite her.

"Now listen, bitch! That coffee's the last thing I am ever going to do for you. There will be an initial period whilst I teach you to cook to a certain standard, how I like the house kept immaculate, and I will even show you how to keep the pools clean. On any given night when I require sex, I will inform you at dinner and after you have cleaned the dishes, you will come to my bedroom, Matt Dawson style. You are never going to leave the house. I have every door and window wired up with explosives and if you attempt to leave, you will not only be scarred again, you will be blown to bits. Do you understand?"

Olivia could only look at Phil with a look of abject fear. She knew it was no accident that night and she could still smell the flesh on her face burning. The worm had truly turned.

The Missing Boy

Lynda White was fourteen today, the twenty-sixth of June 1990. Her mum had promised her a birthday tea where she could invite her two best friends from school, Molly and Annie, and her friend Sally who lived next door. The only downside was her two brothers, Alan and Billy, would have to be there. As a bonus, Lynda had badgered her mum all week asking if she could go to the annual funfair and her mum finally agreed when she insisted that Lynda take the boys. Her mum was going to drop them off at 2pm and, after doing the weekly grocery shop, would pick them up at 4pm. Her mum's parting words to Lynda were, "Whatever you do, Lynda, look after the boys. Don't let them out of your sight for one minute."

Lynda fully intended to do that. Her Mum had given her ten pounds, enough for two rides each, and some candy floss and a drink.

Lynda loved the atmosphere of the funfair. The noise of the crowd, the cries of "Come on down kids, try your luck!" Lynda ignored that vender as she didn't think her mum would be too pleased to find out the boys had been shooting air rifles, no matter how big the prize.

Lynda, holding Alan's hand, who was holding Billy's hand, gravitated to the waltzer. It soared around and around, up and down, and although they played really old Rock'n Roll records, they played them really loud, which only added to the atmosphere.

Alan was tugging Lynda's hand. "I want to go on the carousel, please, please."

It was then that Lynda spotted him, Scruff McKinnon, a lad from the year above at school, the coolest guy in all the school. They called him 'Scruff' because he was always immaculate in his freshly-washed and ironed chinos. His Calvin Klein t-shirt and a pair of the latest trainers made him stand out from the crowd. The truth was Scruff could wear a bin Bag over his head and he still would look the business.

Scruff stopped to talk to her. Lynda was flabbergasted as she had always fancied him. In fact, every girl in school fancied him.

"Yes, that's right. What are you doing here?"

What a dumb question but Scruff replied. "I work here, taking the money on the waltzers."

Scruff coolly stepped onto the flying waltzer and spun the nearest cage around, making the two girls riding the waltzer scream even louder.

Scruff bent over and took a pound coin off both girls and moved on to the next carriage. He was moving effortlessly and Lynda just couldn't keep her eyes off him.

The ride finished and Scruff walked over to Lynda.

"Fancy a free ride?"

Lynda looked down at Alan. "Alan, don't move from here and keep hold of Billy's hand, O.K?"

Alan nodded looking forlornly over at the carousel.

Lynda gazed up at Scruff's blue eyes as he led her by the hand and sat her down. Sitting next to her he said, "I better sit next to you on this ride as it goes pretty fast."

Lynda was in heaven as Scruff held her hand with his left and put his right arm around her to keep her safe. Lynda didn't notice Alan and Billy wandering off.

Alan was captivated by the carousel and stood watching it. Billy just sat down on the grass bored.

"I want an ice cream," said Billy.

"Wait until Lynda has finished. I cannot get you an ice cream as she has the money."

'Do you want to go on the carousel, son?" A strange man with a squinty eye had bent down to talk to Alan.

"I can't, I've got no money, and I have to watch my little brother."

"No problem," said Squinty. "The first ride is free and I'll look after your little brother for you."

'Would you?" Alan's reply excitedly.

"Of course I will, son." Squinty lifted Alan onto the carousel, waited for it to start moving and, looking down at Billy said, "Do you want an ice cream, son?"

Young Billy enthusiastically nodded his head and held the man's hand whilst they walked away to find the ice cream stall.

Lynda was on the waltzer, Alan was on the carousel.

Lynda, Alan, their mum and Dad never saw Billy again.

***

Squint had finished his work setting up the stalls that day at noon and was back in his caravan heating up some beans for his lunch, to put with the two slices of bread already in the toaster, when there was a loud and ominous knock on his caravan door, a knock he hadn't heard for quite some time.

The gentleman who entered was well over six-foot tall, well-dressed, and spoke in a well-educated accent. "Well Squinty, old chap, we meet again."

"I told you the last time I wasn't going to do nuffin' for you again."

"Oh! So you didn't spend the five hundred quid I gave you?"

Squinty had a flashback of a disastrous day at the races where every sure-fire winner came in last and left him skint again.

"That didn't last me very long. It's not worth it for the risk."

"We need another 'package' for tonight. The boys, well you cannot really call them boys, can you, need a nights entertainment. I've fixed the champagne. I've fixed the smoke salmon and caviar, and just need you to provide the dessert."

"The last time I did it, it was early evening in December at the Christmas fare. The little boy didn't recognise me because it was too dark."

"Anyway, he was in such a state. When you brought him back, I had to take him straight to the nearest hospital and left him on their doorstep."

Squinty looked down at the floor. "I heard he was in hospital for weeks and he's still not right after what you lot did to him."

Squint didn't see the blow coming. The backhander knocked him clean off his feet and he crashed into his television, smashing it into pieces.

"Have the 'package' tonight at the usual place at eight o'clock sharp or else! I have some very important guests attending tonight, a special ring of people if you get my drift. We've even got the local M.P. coming. However, I'm a fair man. As you are taking a bigger risk there will a thousand ponds in an envelope when the package is returned. O.K?"

Squint just looked up with his good eye focused with hatred.

"Don't even think of letting me down Squinty boy as you know what'll happen to you if you don't deliver."

All hell broke loose at the fairground when it got round that a little boy was missing.

"How old is he?"

"What colour hair?"

"What was he wearing?"

It was Scruff who took control by calling the police.

Alan was sobbing in Lynda's arms and Lynda was staring out into the distance not acknowledging anything the police were asking her. They managed to get a description from Scruff who seemed to be the only one who was capable of helping the police. He told the police that the last time anyone saw Billy was when he was standing next to the carousel with Alan. The police shut down the fairground and told no one to leave. It was a huge task interviewing, on site, over a hundred fairground goers, along with the staff that worked there.

Squint was drinking a large whisky when the police knocked on his caravan door. He opened the top half, as he didn't want the policeman to see the smashed television in the corner of the living area. He leant out, and asked what was going on.

The young policeman took his name, confirmed the caravan was his permanent address, and wrote down on his notebook that Squint stated he had been in his caravan all afternoon after a hard mornings work. Thank God the policeman didn't go any further and search the bedroom as Billy was lying under the duvet on the bed. The little lad was still asleep from the chloroform Squint had swiftly administered when Billy realised he wouldn't be getting an ice cream in the back of Squint's caravan.

The policeman told Squint as a matter of procedure, they would like him to attend an identity parade at the local police station the following morning at 10am and the missing lad's sister and brother would be attending to try and pick out who took Billy as it had to be either a customer at the fairground or one of the workers.

Squint said he would attend and added that he would do anything to help find the young lad.

After the policeman left, Squint sighed a huge sigh of relief, sat down with his whiskey, and tried to work out how he was going to get the 'package' to its destination by eight o'clock that evening.

The answer came in a rather large laundry basket from the room where the wives did their washing and ironing. He just walked in, picked up the basket, went back to the caravan, placed the boy in it, and covered him with his duvet.

If he was stopped, he was going to tell whoever it was he was going to the local launderette as normal, as washing hadn't removed a large coffee stain he had spilt whilst drinking in bed.

Squint loaded his van and, after a successful delivery, he just sat up all night, staring into space, waiting for that dreaded knock. Sometime during the night, he thought he heard someone tampering with his van. Upon inspection, he could see nothing in the darkness, so he closed the door of the caravan and thought nothing else of it.

It was midnight when Squint heard the sound of a car engine pull up outside his caravan. He opened the door to see two men. One was carrying the laundry basket, which he put down beside the caravan steps, the other man just handed Squint an envelope. Without a word, both men got into the car and slowly drove away into the night.

Squint opened the envelope to find a thousand pounds in fifty pound notes. He looked down at the laundry basket and was nearly sick at what he saw. The duvet, when it left Squint earlier on that evening, was white. Now it was red and white. Huge patches of blood. When Squint looked inside, he could clearly see the five year old lad was dead. No wonder the two men had left sharpish. What the hell to do now?

The other people who didn't sleep that night were Lynda's and Alan's mum and dad. The dad just sat around the dinner table. He was a hard-working clean-living man who had never drank, and was nursing a now empty bottle of whisky someone got them for Christmas. Even after drinking the whole bottle, it did nothing to dullen his pain. Lynda and her mum were inconsolable. Lynda was still staring into space in a state of complete shock. She hadn't said a word to anybody since coming off the waltzer. Lynda's mum was sobbing like a child and had been crying from the moment the young police woman knocked on their door to say they still hadn't found Billy but they would carry on the search in the morning. She told them that the television response to the appeal to help find Billy had been brilliant with hundreds of people pledging their support and they would be there the next day to help with the search.

***

Squint wasn't the most intelligent of men but, like most small-time criminals, he could be devious when the time called for it. There was a lorry that carried the generator next to Squint's caravan with a huge tractor-type wheel and tyre bolted onto the back of the machine as a spare in case they ever had a puncture travelling from one site to another. Squint unbolted the wheel and using all of his strength carried it into his caravan. The wheel just fitted into the width of the caravan door.

He got his toolbox out of his van, took it into the caravan, and proceeded to take the tyre off. First of all, he had to depressurise it and then, using the tyre wrench, was able to take the tyre off one side of the wheel. Squint sat and had a rest to prepare himself for the task he definitely wasn't looking forward to. Now to put the body into the wheel.

Squint wasn't to know how clever he had been. After squeezing the small body around the curve of the wheel, he was able to replace the tyre and pump enough air into it to take it back to its normal pressure, thirty-three and a third pounds per square inch. The clever thing that Squinty wasn't aware of was the vacuum this created meant that the body would not decompose, or smell, and would not give off any tell-tale signs for a very long time.

After replacing the wheel onto the back of the lorry, Squint packed up all of his belongings and took them into his van. He then drove away, very slowly, into a dark, cloudy rain-filled night to make his escape, to where, he did not know.

Perhaps it was the constant fall of the heavy rain, or the fact he didn't know the road well, but Squint didn't see the one in six sign at the side of the road indicating he was approaching a steep hill.

Everything was fine until the van reached the sixty miles per hour mark and Squinty pressed his brake pedal to slow down. The van slowed a little bit but when Squinty pressed the brake pedal again, nothing happened. He then, in a panic, pressed the brake pedal all the way to the floor. The van had no brakes!

Two things then happened. Firstly, he realised someone had been tampering with his brakes earlier that night as they were now useless and secondly, as he tried to maintain the balance of the vehicle going around a corner at the bottom of the hill, he only succeeded in completely losing control as the van mounted the kerb and crashed into a road sign. The electronic sign which was supposed to show a smiley face and print out 'well done' if you were going less than the thirty mile an hour speed limit now showed a decidedly unhappy face as it appeared to look down at the body that had been flung through the windscreen and was laying across the other side of the road minus its head.

As luck would have it, it was the same young constable who had spoken to Squint about the identity parade who was called out to attend the road accident on Shakespeare Hill just outside of town. The young lad had the gruesome task of retrieving the head and placing it with the body when the ambulance turned up. He recognised that it was Squinty and wondered why the van was full of his belongings and why he was obviously driving somewhere in the middle of the night when he was supposed to be attending the identity parade at the local police station in the morning.

W.P.C. Sheila Ferguson, the family liaison officer who was tasked to stay with Lynda, Alan, and their mum and dad, got Alan to speak about what happened as, once again, there was no joy in getting Lynda to respond to questioning. Alan said the man was friendly as he promised him an ice cream after the ride on the carousel. He also noticed that the man had a squinty eye which made his face look kind of funny.

It wasn't long before this report and the report from the road accident pointed the finger firmly at Squinty being responsible for the kidnapping of young Billy. But where was the young lad? The C.I.D. sergeant in charge of the case cancelled the identity parade and concentrated on organising the hundreds of volunteers to search every blade of grass around the fairground and surrounding fields for any clues. They also searched all the caravans, wash house and toilets.

The only thing they found was in Squinty's caravan. It was a metal shaped 'S' with bits of coloured material attached to it. Billy's mum and dad recognised the remains. It came from the belt buckle on Billy's trousers. This proved to the police that Billy had actually been in Squint's caravan but where was Billy? Where had he been taken?

***

26th June 2020

It was Linda's 44th birthday. Alan and Lynda never celebrated it. Every year they went to their hometown where the annual fairground was held. They just sat in the car and looked at the carousel going around, hearing the music blaring out from the speakers surrounding the waltzer. Alan hugged Lynda as the tears ran down her face.

Five years ago, on the 25th anniversary, they did two things. They bought some flowers. The people enjoying the fairground entertainment must have thought it strange when a couple placed the flowers next to the carousel, stood back, and leaning against the spare wheel of the generator lorry, just stood together in each other's arms. The lady cried and the man stared at the flowers with a look of complete sadness.

Alan and Lynda weren't to know it but the spare wheel they leant against that day was brand new as the original spare wheel had replaced a punctured one whilst the fairground lorry was driving down the M1 to their next venue.

The next thing they did that day was to go to the nearest police station to give their fingerprints and D.N.A. so their details could be put onto the national database. That way if Billy was ever found and his D.N.A. was taken, there would be a match and they would know it was their long lost brother.

It seemed like yesterday as Alan and Lynda thought back to that fateful day. Was it really thirty years ago?

A lot had happened in that time. Their father was the first to go. He moved to London and ended up on the streets. He was finally finished off by the copious amounts of alcohol consumed and suffered a massive heart attack in a shop-way where he had been sleeping for the night.

The news was too much for their mum to bear. She couldn't cope anymore and committed suicide by jumping in front of a train. Alan and Lynda both carried on as they still had slim hopes that Billy might still be alive. They ploughed all their efforts into their careers. Alan's Master's Degree in forensic science paved the way for a career in the police force. If any child was reported missing, Alan always asked his boss if he could be assigned to the case as they could use his personal experience.

One year, helping with a search, he found a credit card near to where the little girl in the case had last been seen. The police traced the owner of the credit card and whilst raiding the man's house, were able to rescue the little girl who was bound and gagged. Alan was promoted for this, amongst other achievements, and was assigned to security at

Number 10 Downing Street. Alan was pleased as he would be working alongside Lynda who would be working in the office next to Alan. Lynda's Ph.D in Politics gave her the position of P.A. to the Prime Minister of the day. There was excitement in the office as a new Prime Minister had just been elected. A former Mayor of London, he was known for his charisma and big personality. Lynda was particularly pleased as the last one had been a bit of a bore.

It was on the first day of working together when they received some terrible news. There had been an accident the week before on the M25 between a family car and a fairground lorry. The family in the car had no chance as the lorry had suffered a puncture, careered onto the oncoming traffic, and completely wiped out a Ford Galaxy with two adults and three children on board. The lorry was deemed to be overweight as it carried a large generator used to supply electricity to all the fairground rides. The fairground worker, who was driving, survived with concussion and a broken leg. Upon inspection of the lorry the motorway police discovered a horrific sight. The punctured tyre had been ripped from the rear wheel but there was something inside. It was the partly decomposed body of a small child, sex to be determined. The remains were taken straight away to the forensic science department. It had taken a week to fully determine the facts surrounding what was now known to be a young boy.

Immediately on hearing the news, Alan left the office and made his way to the mortuary where the body was being kept. His experience and knowledge in forensic science would be invaluable in helping identify the body. All the way there, Alan's stomach was tightened in knots. What if it was Billy? How could he tell Lynda? The doctor on duty that day was Jack Thomas, an old university pal of Alan. Although they hadn't seen each other in years, Alan's only opening word was "Well?"

"You'd better sit down, Alan."

Alan looked up at Jack's face. "Oh my God, it's Billy, isn't it?"

Jack slowly nodded his head. "We've got a 99.9% match on the D.N.A."

Alan had been dreading this moment for over thirty years and he was at the point where there were no more tears. He had strengthened his heart to this news years ago.

He needed to know how Billy died and who was responsible for his body spending years packed inside a tyre.

"Do you know how he died?" Alan pleaded.

"Alan, there's something else you should know."

Alan looked puzzled. Surely things couldn't be any worse.

"We found additional and different D.N.A. inside the body"

"What?" cried Alan.

"There's no easy way to tell you this, but Billy had been raped."

Now the tears flowed. Alan could only say "Why?"

After thirty years of not knowing, it was too much for Alan and he collapsed.

James called for the medics and there was a swift response. They loaded a semi-conscious Alan onto a stretcher. James was dreading answering any more of Alan's questions. He was relieved he didn't have to describe the horrific injuries the lad must have suffered before he died.

***

Alan insisted that it would only be Lynda and himself at the funeral. As Alan watched the coffin move off to be cremated, he thought there was only one thing worse than watching a full-size coffin moving forward to be burnt and that was the sight of a small child's coffin. They both broke down and sobbed. Both their hearts were completely broken.

The media made the most of it. There were plenty of stories in the tabloids about a young dead body incarcerated inside a lorry tyre. As usual, there was no consideration for the family. Was the young lad dead before he was put into the tyre? How did he die? Who was responsible for this horrendous act? The newspapers and television lapped it up.

Lynda had a small photo of Billy on her desk. Next to it was a small framed print of Billy's D.N.A. Two long, thin strands twisted around each other like a spiral staircase. Next to that was the D.N.A. of the person who had raped Billy. Lynda knew every detail of this particular D.N.A. She was granted permission from the police to trawl through the D.N.A. profile of every known sex offender going back fifty years.

The machine that they had given her enabled her to study individual D.N.A. samples. Lynda stayed in her office many late nights, sometimes until midnight, going through tens of thousands sex offenders' D.N.A.s. It was going to take her years. She knew if she found a matching D.N.A. to that of Billy's, they will have caught the culprit

Lynda started a campaign to encourage every person in the U.K. to give their D.N.A. to the D.N.A. database. There was a massive response. Thousand more crimes would be solved. There would be no doubt in murder cases. It would reduce crime when the criminal fraternity knew there was no chance of getting away with their crimes if their D.N.A. was on the national and European database. Unfortunately, there was always the opposition that would disagree and argue that it was against their 'human rights' and people should be given the basic human right of privacy. There is a law in the U.K. which states that if you get 100,000 signatures, the House of Commons are legally bound to debate your petition in Parliament.

Lynda started an online petition. Within two weeks, she had over 100,000 signatures. On the day of the discussion, Parliament put the proposal last on the list for the day to debate so everyone could watch B.B.C. Parliament when they got home from work, as the proposal, and the circumstances around it, had captured the nation's imagination. If the motion was successful, there would be a delay before the proposal could be brought before the House in the shape of an actual Parliamentary Act but the Prime Minister, always quick to see an opportunity, announced that he would get his fingerprints taken, along with his D.N.A. taken and added to the database.

Lynda was working late on the evening the Prime Minister was to release his D.N.A. details. Alan was working in his office next door. The forensic team, who had taken the P.M.'s samples earlier in the day, returned and asked if they could borrow Lynda's machine so they could magnify the samples so they could take a clear picture, with the best quality possible, for the television cameras. The camera was set up to show the P.M. at his desk ready to talk to the nation. Alan came through to Lynda's office to watch the programme on her office computer which was tuned to the B.B.C. channel which was transmitting the programme.

Very experienced with the media, the P.M. looked directly at the camera. "Hello, and good evening to everyone. When I was voted your Prime Minister, one of my party's main platforms was to reduce the level of crime in this country, particularly the horrific rise in knife crime. Tonight, I am going to show you the recent result of my fingerprints taken today along with a sample of my D.N.A. I have no problem with this as I wholeheartedly support the Act which will pave the way for every child at birth to have his or her D.N.A. taken as well as the rest of the population. So, without further ado, this is what my finger prints look like." A caption came onto the screen clearly showing the P.M.'s fingerprint which was actually his left thumb. "And the next caption will show my D.N.A."

At first, Lynda couldn't believe what she saw. The Prime Minister's D.N.A. matched the D.N.A. of the person who had raped Billy. Alan didn't know there was anything wrong until Lynda turned to him and let out the most horrific scream. "It's him!" she cried.

Alan was totally shocked. What the hell was going on!

"It's him, he's the murdering bastard!"

With that, Lynda burst into the P.M.'s office, passed the bewildered television crew, threw herself onto the P.M.'s desk and was able to scratch his face and start punching him before anybody could react.

"You scum, you murdering scum!"

Lynda had the strength of a mad woman. The P.M. was too shocked to reply or do anything. He vainly tried to protect himself. All the time this was happening, it was being broadcast on B.B.C. World all over the planet.

Alan had recovered his senses and dashed into the room and managed to drag Lynda from the P.M. before she did actually kill him as, by this time, she had both hands around his neck to strangle him. Two security guys responded as the P.M. managed to press the alarm button below his desk and they swiftly took Lynda away from the office to a more secure place whilst everybody tried to find out what was happening. Alan went back into Lynda's office, rewound the programme until it got to the part of the D.N.A. sample being shown on the screen. He studied the sample next to Billy's D.N.A.

"Bloody hell, she's right. He is a murdering paedophile."

He then did something he thought he would never have to do in a million years.

He went next door and arrested the Prime Minister of Great Britain.

Reunited

Malden's skin had a very light bluish tint. Unlike the rare female species, his body still had a few strands of hair, a throwback from when the species depended on their body hair to keep them warm against the outside elements.

Malden often wondered what it had been like on the outside. The species had been forced underground after the holocaust had completely devastated the planet. The outside had been rendered inhabitable thus the great underground cities had been built with the long connecting tunnels stretching great distances beneath the crust of the planet.

Malden discarded the telepathic pictures of the ancient cities his mind had projected onto the huge computer screen that took up all of one side of his room. His square room was only part of a huge honeycomb of rooms that made up the underground world of his species.

The room was bare-looking. A blueish ultra violet light glowed from the top of the room. On the opposite wall there was another screen. This was his life support, educational and leisure video computer. If Malden felt sick, or was hungry, or needed anything, he simply applied his thought transference technique to the computer and his wishes were obeyed.

Using the same method of telepathy, he could

instruct the video computer to show pictures of ancient art, fill the room with any type of music, from electronic to classical, and use the computer to contact any other individuals who also lived in their square rooms. He had, in fact, used this method once to communicate with the female that had given birth to him, but that was a long time ago. He was the twenty-third birth child so it was difficult for her to remember anything about him. Thus, he only contacted her that one time.

Feeling bored, Malden's brain switched on the 'Daily Occurrence' early morning programme to catch up on any overnight news. The elders were giving a lecture on the process of body elimination. It was stated that one of the elders had existed for some time without his body by means of linking his mind to the automatic life support system. This computer gave them the oxygen they needed and took away their body wastes during their sleep and corrected any problems within their body to prevent illness. The average age of the species was nearly two hundred years and the elders were trying to perfect a system where, without the physical body holding them back, they could live forever.

Malden shivered involuntarily. Although he admitted that he had no longer any use for his body, he was strangely disturbed at the thought of existing without it. It seemed others felt the same as a protest had been made to the elders from quite a number of other individuals. Malden decided to keep his thoughts to himself as it had been known in the past that too much opposition to the elders could result in banishment to the outside world, and that meant only one thing, certain death. The elders stated that banishment to the outside was a good thing for their society. It controlled the exploding population and improved the quality of the species.

Suddenly, the picture on the video computer vanished, the blueish light faded from the room, and the hum of the life support system died away. Malden's reaction to this was too simply switch his thoughts to summon the Automatic Repair Robot. He had summoned the A.R.R. once before when there had been a fault in the Central Computer so there was no real cause for him to worry.

However, after half an hour, Malden began to panic. The A.R.R. had not arrived and the air in the room was beginning to run out. The blue light went out completely leaving Malden to grope blindly looking for the door. He had only been through the door once when he was brought to the room as a child and he was unsure where the door led to. When he finally found it, the faulty computer was unable to open the door. No matter how many times he applied his thought commands, the door stayed firmly closed.

He then remembered the emergency door lever. Groping around, he tried pitting his pitiful strength against it but nothing happened. It would not move. Trickles of perspiration stinging his opaque skin, Malden tried to exert his flabby muscles to greater effort. At last, he felt the lever move and with one final mighty effort, the door opened. Malden greedily breathed in the air of the passageway and was filled with a strange exhilaration of achievement.

Malden followed the passageway hoping to find a repair robot to enable him to put his world back together again. Struggling along the dark passageway, Malden suddenly bumped into another individual. Unable to see Malden's mind, he asked the other individual if his room had malfunctioned. He got no response. Without aid of the computer, his telepathic powers were non-existent.

Malden put forward his hands to try to convey some sort of sign. He was met with the soft touch of flesh. The individual was one of the rare female of the species, distinguished by a softer and smoother texture of the skin. Malden felt a strange feeling pass through his body at the warm touch of her hand.

"I am Selvka."

Malden recoiled. She had spoken in the ancient manner. The sound of her voice had startled him. It was not the mechanical sound the computer used to relate his thoughts to the elders but a sound filled with feeling and life. Through his studies, he understood the female he was unable to speak the ancient language as he had always used his mind to communicate.

"If you understand, touch me."

Malden reached out and once again enjoyed the sensation of touch.

"Our life support systems have failed. We shall die unless we find new air. Follow me."

Malden held onto the female's hand and stumbled after her along the dark passageway. Hour after hour they travelled with the air getting thinner and more foul to breathe.

Then suddenly a strange sensation came over his body. He started to shiver and struck out with his hands to stop this substance from affecting him.

"We are safe. Cold air is blowing down onto us from this ventilation shaft."

Malden breathed deeply at the fresh air and no longer struggled against it blowing against his body.

As he followed Selvka up the ventilation shaft, he was filled with fear of the destination she might be leading him to. Up and up they climbed until they finally emerged at the top of the shaft. Malden's eyes were practically blinded by a strange and powerful light. He felt Selvka's arms around him as she continued to lead him onwards. When they finally stopped, Malden, exhausted from all of the unaccustomed effort, lay on the ground and fell into a deep sleep.

***

On awakening, Malden opened his eyes expecting to see the neon blue light of his room. Instead, he saw a black roof with millions of tiny dots on it with a ball of light in the middle. Malden sat up frightened and looked around him. There were giant plants reaching towards the black roof like the ones he had saw on the computer when he watched programmes about the ancient times before the holocaust. The floor he was sitting on was damp and unfamiliar.

"You are on the outside."

Malden turned and saw Selvka walking towards him.

"It is night on the outside so your eyes will not need protecting. Stand up and look around you. See how beautiful the outside is. We have plants to eat and rivers to drink from. Look at the stars and the trees. Breathe in the clean air.

Selvka hesitated, before adding, "There has been a massive power surge in the underworld. All of the mainframe computers have been damaged irrevocably. We have no idea how many souls have perished. You are one of the lucky ones who we have managed to rescue."

Malden could not understand, the underworld meant life, the outside meant death.

Selvka pointed to a red glow on the horizon. "There lies all that is left of the nuclear holocaust. Nature has conquered it and in a few hundred more years, the last areas of the deadly rays will be gone. The elders banished our people to the underworld to meet our death but instead, the outside has given us new life."

Selvka took Malden's hand and lead him to her people.

The Kidnapper

When he awoke, it was pitch black, very cold, and as he automatically felt his crotch, he was wet. He started to cry as he knew his mum would be angry and she would tell him off for wetting himself. As he tried to look around, all he could remember was sliding down the slide at the playground and a cloth being put over his mouth. He thought someone was playing and it was part of a game. He remembered the smell of the cloth, a strong smell that made him dizzy. He remembered no more. In between sobs, he tried shouting for help. The echo of his young voice reverberated around the curves of the tunnel he was in. There was no reply.

After a while, the darkness gave way to a small round hole of light above his head and, as his eyes adjusted, he was able to see he was in a small round area that stretched quite a distance to the top where the small round hole was. To the side of him was a coiled rope which was attached to his waist. In the corner of his small round room was a stream of water which he gratefully scooped up and drank as he was very, very thirsty.

He arranged the rope into a pile that he could sit on to make himself more comfortable. He lay down on the rope and cried himself to sleep.

A noise of footsteps above awakened him. A cry of "Look out below!" and a clattering followed by a splash as a yellow object landed in the stream of water. The sound of the footsteps diminished leaving only the trickle of the stream to break the silence. He looked over at the yellow object. It was a bunch of bananas. He tore one from the bunch, peeled it, and with great hunger, ate it quickly. He didn't eat anymore. There were four left and he didn't know when there would be anymore.

He suddenly realised he hadn't called for help when he heard the footsteps. He was determined to shout as loud as he could if there was another visit. He thought perhaps he was stuck in a wishing well. Perhaps a wish would come true so he wished his mum and step-dad were out looking for him as well as his elder brother, Sammy.

It was his Auntie Jean who was looking after him in the swing park as it was Wednesday and his mum worked on a Wednesday so, in the holidays from school, he spent all day with his Auntie until his step-dad, Papa Jon, came to pick him up from his Auntie's house. He always liked it when Papa Jon picked him as they always went for ice cream.

"Don't tell your mum, this is our little secret" somehow made the ice creams taste better. He had never known his real dad and, even though he was his step-dad, he loved his Papa Jon with all of his heart.

As the day went on, the light at the top of the tunnel became brighter. He stood and felt all around where he was sitting. The wall was made of bricks and he was able to climb a little way up, as some of the cement between the bricks had worn away, and he was able to get a handhold in some and a foothold in another. He was about six feet up when he slipped and fell. Luckily, he landed on the coiled rope which softened his fall but it still gave him a real scare. He started to think of his mum and Papa Jon out looking for him and he started to cry. To cheer himself up, he ate one more of his bananas and hungrily slurped some of the fresh water from the stream. He was five years old.

***

Papa Jon had a feeling that his stepson had been kidnapped when he arrived at the swing park only to be greeted by a sobbing sister-in-law being held tightly by a young woman police constable. The police had already organised a local search which Jon quickly joined in. The reason why he felt that his stepson, little Jimmy, had been snatched was that Jon was a multi-millionaire and had always dreaded something like this would happen. His house had sixteen security cameras outside with four secretly placed inside. All the internal doors of his big beautiful house were painted with a mahogany veneer and looked fabulous when, in fact, all the doors were made of solid steel. There was a 'panic room' that only he knew about which had been built into the house. It took Jon twenty minutes overnight to lock up and set the cameras to a fresh recording position and all twenty were connected directly to the nearest police station.

Jon was worried sick. It had started raining heavily and all he could think about was where was little Jimmy. He prayed he was safe somewhere. He slept fitfully that first night. He would not have slept at all if he knew that Jimmy was unable to sleep on his coiled rope bed as he was standing and sobbing in twelve inches of water which was getting deeper by the hour.

"Jimmy, Jimmy!" shouted the man's voice. Jimmy had heard the footsteps and had cried loudly for help. The rain had stopped during the night and the rising water had subsided.

"Look out below!" the voice cried. Jimmy curled himself into a little ball as the clattering and loud splash indicated that another delivery of bananas had been made. He finished the first batch the day before so he quickly devoured two bananas. Once again, he lay on his bed of coiled rope and cried softly looking longingly at the small circle of light far above his head. He felt so scared and alone.

***

Jon decided from the start he would not involve the police. He had openly lied to his wife when promising he would tell them everything as soon as anything happened. The police would know best. They had specialist people who had handled situations like this many times before. This had calmed his wife down a little and with the aid of the doctor-prescribed Valium, she was now soundly asleep.

He would, like he had done all of his life, handle anything that came along himself. He couldn't care less if the kidnapper got away scot-free. All he could think about was getting little Jimmy back in one piece and he was prepared to do whatever it took to make that happen.

It came as no surprise when his landline at home rang at 3am. The voice was obviously spoken through an electronic device to avoid detection and, strangely enough, was recorded giving Jon no chance to respond or negotiate.

"£100K by tomorrow. I will call your mobile when the banks close."

This posed two questions to Jon. How the hell was he going to put together £100K by close of play tomorrow and how the hell did the kidnapper know his mobile number?

***

Little Jimmy had decided to go into 'the big bath' as his mum used to call it. He took all of his clothes off and, and still unable to untie the knot that held the rope around his waist, he crawled over to the stream and lay in it even though it was really cold, and he had an all over wash. He lay on the coiled rope until he was dry and then put his clothes back on. He kept his shoes and socks off because tomorrow, when it got light, he was going to have another go at climbing out of this nightmare he was living in.

***

Next day, Jon got up early and was knocking on his local NatWest door asking to see the manager when they opened at 9am.

"Ah! Mr. Henderson, what can I do for you today?"

Tom Russel, the newly-promoted bank manager, was young and ambitious and easily fell for Jon's patter that he needed a £50K cash loan, today, to tie up a very sweet deal with some Russian contacts Jon had in the property world. Tom explained it was very unusual, but Jon was a valued customer and the Discretionary Limit on his account was £50K. Jon already knew this and that was the reason he only asked for £50K instead of the full £100K.

He left the bank with £50K in fifty pound notes in his briefcase. Now how was he going to get the rest? He'd put a call into his best mate, Billy Masson, a car dealer, who always seemed to have wads of cash on him. Billy returned the call and said, without asking why Jon wanted the money, he could only raise £20K.

"That's brilliant, Billy, I'll come to the garage straight away."

After picking up the money from Billy, who raised his hand and shook his head when Jon asked him if he wanted to know what he needed the money for, Jon was able to go back to his bank and draw £10K on his credit card which still left him with a further £20K to find. The only other thing he could think was a Cash Converter store in the nearby city of Leicester. Perhaps they would give him some cash for his gold Rolex he constantly wore on his left wrist.

The owner of the Cash Converter shop kept Jon waiting whilst he established that the Rolex wasn't a fake. He had been done once before when a guy presented him with an Omega Speedmaster and to this day, he thought was genuine. It was only when he sent it away to be cleaned and serviced was he told it was a fake. That little deal had cost him a couple of grand.

Eventually, he came through to the shop floor and announced that Jon's Rolex was genuine and asked Jon if he did really pay twenty-five grand for it when it was new.

'It was a present from my wife for my fortieth birthday," replied Jon thinking back to happier days.

"I can offer you the twenty grand you want. Fifties OK?"

Jon nodded and opened his briefcase.

"You have one month to pay the full amount back and the A.R.P. interest is twenty percent. Obviously, it's in your interest to pay back the loan A.S.A.P."

Jon returned home to await the kidnapper's next call.

When he opened the front door, all hell let loose.

"Where the hell have you been today? Why haven't you answered my calls? The police are here to ask you questions. They should all be out looking for little Jimmy but no, you've been swanning around God knows where and I've been making sodding tea all day while the officers just sit on their backsides."

Jon held her tight as she hammered his chest and finally collapsed in tears.

Police Sergeant Ron Wilson was an experienced officer in missing persons. He tried to come across in a calm and soothing manner but his intuition nagged at him. Here was a dad, not even a dad, a step-dad, whose stepson was missing and he had been out of touch all day.

"Well, Mr. Henderson, can we just start by asking you for your whereabouts yesterday when Jimmy was first reported missing?"

"I was at my office working. I have eleven building sites on the go in various stages of completion and I'm trying to project manage every one of them. You'd be surprised at what goes missing from building sites if strict control is not enforced."

"I can conclude, sir, that you are a man of considerable worth, are you not? Do you think this factor might have anything to do with your stepson missing?"

"What do you mean? Are you implying little Jimmy might have been kidnapped?"

"It's one of the avenues we have to consider, sir."

"But surely we would have heard from someone if that had been the case?" asked Jon.

"O.K., let's move on to today. Your stepson is reported to the police as missing and you, instead of being available to help in our enquiries, are non-contactable and do not reply to the many messages the police, and your wife, have left on your mobile phone. Why is that?"

"Today is wages day. I had to go to the bank to withdraw sufficient funds to pay nearly one hundred wage packets today. There was a problem at the bank in the end so I had to use my credit card as can be easily checked by your officers."

Jon told the police about his visits to the bank but decided not to tell them about his visit to the Cash Converters.

Jon could tell that the policeman was not happy with his replies and as Sergeant Wilson left, he turned and said in a stern voice, "Please stay home tomorrow, sir. I need you at the end of a phone in case there is any news about your missing stepson."

Jon's wife was in bits and, claiming he had a migraine, Jon went to bed early. He didn't want anyone overhearing his next conversation with the kidnapper.

***

Jimmy was doing better on his second attempt at getting out of the well. He climbed up the other side where there were more nooks and crannies. The walls were drier and with more handholds, he was making good progress. The same as most five year olds, he had no fear and was doing really well until it started to rain heavily once again. The next hand hole was too slippy to risk so little Jimmy just held on only for the water running down the sides of the wishing well to wash him away. His fall was from a much higher height than the one before and as he landed heavily, he cracked his head on the ground. He lay there unconscious with blood trickling from a wound in his head making its way into the stream which was steadily rising as the pouring rain continued to fall.

***

The next call from the kidnapper came at four in the morning. Jon had his phone on silent and quickly made his way downstairs to listen to the message.

"Leave a bag with the money inside the yellow recycling bin at the back of Sainsbury's on Green Street at 6am this morning then walk away.

Do not linger as I will then pick up the bag, check the money is correct, and I will text you the G.P.S. co-ordinates where your stepson is being kept."

His wife came into the kitchen.

"Christ, you gave me a fright, Babe!"

"What are you up to, Jon?"

"Nothing, just getting a glass of water."

With that, he went back to bed and lay awake waiting for the bedside clock to read 5:30 a.m. when he would get up, dress and make his way to the local Sainsbury's.

He told his wife that he was going for a drive to clear his head and he would be right back.

There was only a road sweeper dressed in a yellow hi-vis jacket and wearing a black woolly balaclava to keep warm working at the front of Sainsbury's as Jon drove round to the back. He got out of his car. He noticed there was no C.C.T.V. camera's covering the rear of the property.

He took one last look round and deposited the bag of money into the top of the rather full yellow recycling bin, then quickly drove off as instructed. He had left the area so he didn't see the road sweeper go around to the back of the building and retrieve the money.

The sharp shrill single note of his smart phone told him he had a message. There were just two pieces of information. Latitude: 52 degrees 37 minutes 20.03 North. Longitude -1.Degree 13 minutes 29.93 West. He revved his car to the limit and made his way to Leicester Forest East following the mechanical voice that was giving him directions from his sat nav.

After ten miles, he drove up a long gravel path that led to a disused manor.

"You have arrived at your destination," said the voice from the sat nav.

Part of the east wing of the manor was still standing but the rest was just a pile of rubble. He got out of his car. Where could little Jimmy be? He started to run shouting his name "Jimmy! Jimmy!" Every now and then, he would stop and listen. Then he heard it. "Dad! Dad!" A faint reply but where? He walked through some brambles still shouting Jimmy's name. The replies became louder. He came to what appeared to be a disused well and looked down into it. "Jimmy!" he called.

The small boy was at the end of his tether this time, barely whispering his reply.

"Dad, help me, I'm bleeding."

"Hold on son, I'll be back in a minute with a rope."

Jon ran frantically back to the car, flicked open his boot, and took out a tow rope he kept for emergencies and a powerful torch he used for work.

Back at the well, he swiftly lowered the rope and shouted instructions to Jimmy how to wrap the rope around his body and clip the end of the tow rope to complete the secure knot around his waist. Using his torch, Jon could see his boy was in a bad way.

At first, he gently pulled on the tow rope to get the boy standing.

"Now hold tight onto the rope son. It might hurt for a bit but I'll be as quick as I can pulling you up." Jon heaved and rested, heaved and rested, until the small boys head appeared at the top of the well. Jon finally pulled him clear and hugged him tightly.

"Thank you, God,' was all he could say.

The lad was frozen, soaked through with a head injury. Jon quickly carried him back to his car, removed a car blanket from the boot, and wrapped it around little Jimmy. He laid him on the back seat and, after turning the car heater on full, drove at top speed to Leicester General Hospital, phoning his wife on the way with the good news that Jimmy was alive, safe and well.

***

It took years before little Jimmy, now called 'James', could sleep alone. Jon had put a single bed beside his wife so James would feel safe. His wife always fell asleep touching James to make sure he was there.

Jon paid a visit to the wishing well after the police and press had finished to have another look. He decided against filling it in with concrete. His story to the police was he was looking at the old manor with a view to buy it, knock it down, and develop it for private housing when he heard the cries from the wishing well. James had somehow ended up at the manor and whilst investigating the property, he had come across the wishing well he had accidentally fallen in. James was in no shape to be interviewed by the police in hospital so, as far as the police were concerned, it was case closed.

Throughout James' life, Jon's first priority was James' security. James wore a smart phone so that Jon knew exactly where the young lad was at any given time. When James entered Eton as a boarder, Jon employed a local security company to watch and guard James from a distance if he ever left the school. Jon was paranoid about James's security as he never knew when, if ever, he was going to get another mechanical voice on the end of his phone demanding even more money.

***

James surprised everyone by joining the Royal Marines when he left school. The only problem was during training, he had a severe panic attack when one of the tasks he was asked to perform meant he had to crawl with full pack underwater for twenty yards. He only made the first ten, collapsed on the bank, and lay there sobbing. He was sent to the army hospital for tests. It was whilst he was there that Jon came to visit him.

The kidnap had never been mentioned. Jon wasn't even sure James remembered anything about it. Obviously, the underwater experience had brought it all back from his sub-conscious.

Jon sat on the bed and holding the hand of his eighteen year old stepson, told him what happened in the wishing well all of thirteen years ago.

"I only have memories of being wet and falling from a great height. It is a nightmare I have quite often. I thought it was a dream I made up."

Jon explained it was the reason for the panic attack and told him not to worry about going underwater again.

"There's another thing, James. Your mother and I thought that now you're eighteen, you might want to contact your real father."

With that, Jon pulled out of his wallet a photo of a rather handsome young man looking into the camera with a nice smile on his face but with quite a vivid scar on the left side of his face.

"Now I know where I get my good looks from," said James jokingly.

"How did he get that scar?"

"Brawling in a pub one night. Your Dad liked a drink or three."

"I hope you don't mind me saying this, Jon, but you're my real dad. I have no desire to find a man who left my mum to bring me up alone. Thank God she met you."

***

On James's first leave from the Marines, Jon took him to see the wishing well, told him how he had found him and hoped it would banish James's nightmares once and for all.

Life went on for the family. Jon's business was now listed in the FT 1000 and James had risen to the rank of Captain. He no longer suffered from the nightmare of falling and, since the first one, he hadn't had any more panic attacks. He got his promotion through a successful six months serving in Iraq where he had seen action and was 'mentioned in dispatches'. He was hardened to life as he had seen his best friend being blown up by an I.E.D. James had been instrumental in helping him train for the Paralympics. Jon no longer worried about James's security as many years had passed by without incident.

One day when James was on leave, he was walking along Oxford Street in London on his way to meet the woman who he hoped to be his future wife. He had to walk under a ladder or avoid the scaffolding of some building works, or he had to walk on the busy road.

There was a young mum pushing a pram in front of him having to make the same decision. All of a sudden, James heard a crash and the noise of falling scaffolding. "Look out below!" came the cry of the builder.

James reacted instantly and managed to shove the mother and the pram out of the way only to have a scaffolding pole strike the back of his head. The next thing he knew he was awake in hospital with his head heavily bandaged. His mum was sitting next to his bed and Jon was looking out of the window when James came round.

"Thank God, you're alright," said his mum.

Jon turned around with a grateful smile on his face.

"You did well, Son. It's all over the papers how you saved that young mum's life and the life of her baby."

James just smiled weakly. The nurse looking after him came in to take his blood pressure and temperature and asked politely if they could leave James so he could have a rest. They could come back in the evening.

James lifted his head and waved goodbye. As he lay back, he couldn't get the cry he heard out of his mind, "Look out below!" Where the hell did he know that voice from?

***

James was in hospital for two weeks. Lynda, the girl he was supposed to meet for dinner the day of the accident, had visited him every day and it was obvious to James she was the one. He hoped, with all of his heart, that she felt the same way.

While he was in hospital, James had a lot of time on his hands and he was determined, when he left the hospital, to investigate the building firm that had caused the accident. His mum and dad advised him to take legal action against the company but James was just happy to be alive and wanted to get back on duty with the army. There was a rumour that his regiment was to be deployed to Iraq once again and he didn't want to miss out on the posting, as he felt a great bond with the men he commanded and he didn't want to let them down.

When James got home, one of the first things he did was to switch on his computer to catch up on his e-mails. After trawling through them, he decided to google the company developing the building in Oxford Street and find out who was responsible for the accident.

It came as a surprise to discover the building company's name was the same as his, Henderson. James found the company's website with the strapline 'Henderson Builders, No Job too big, No Job too small." The M.D. of the company was Ray Henderson. It couldn't be, could it? His father's name was Raymond.

He clicked on the name and sure enough, when the picture profile appeared on the screen, the scar gave it away. It was the same photograph Jon had shown him when his parents asked if he wanted to get to know his father.

Raymond Henderson had done well for himself with his own building company. James considered whether to sue, but that meant meeting the man in court. This wasn't something James was prepared to do. He just wanted to get back to his men and carry on doing his duty.

James had a week left of his leave and was determined to spend every minute with Lynda. She was a massive ABBA fan so he booked two tickets to see 'Mamma Mia' and early tickets on the train so they could do some sightseeing in the afternoon before the evening show.

They were walking down Oxford Street when James decided to show Lynda where the accident had happened. When they got there, the building work was nearly completed. The sign above the office block declared proudly 'Henderson Builders' and, on impulse, James decided to go to the site office whilst Lynda had a coffee at the Starbucks across the road from the site.

He knocked on the door.

"Come in!" shouted a voice. James entered the office and came face to face with his father for the first time.

"How can I help you?"

"I'm the man who was hit by the scaffold pole recently."

"Have you come here to tell me you've changed your mind about suing me?"

"No, I've come here to thank the person who shouted "Look out below!"

Without that warning, the lady with the pram and her little one could have died or, at the very least, may have suffered very serious injuries."

"Well, you've come to the right place. It was me who shouted the warning." Raymond Henderson looked really pleased with himself.

"Well thank you, sir! Luck must follow you around. I've read about you, how you started your company with money you won on the lottery, £100K if I remember rightly."

"That's right, young fella. I admit I had a bit of a head start but the company is growing all the time," he boasted.

James thanked Raymond once more and left. He couldn't go straight back to Lynda as his heart had practically stood still. It was one thing seeing your real father for the first time face to face, but it was entirely another matter finding out he was the man who kidnapped you and put you in a deep well, all at the age of five.

He thought about the insurgents he had shot and killed in Iraq. At least they were fighting men, fighting for a cause they believed in. Would any of them do to their sons what Raymond Henderson had done to his son? James thought long and hard about what he should do next. Shooting his father was too quick. He'd have to think of something more fitting.

***

It was exactly a year later when James came back from patrolling a rather nasty part of the Helmand province in Iraq when, after his debrief with his commanding officer, the cry of "Post's Up" cheered him, and all of his men, as the adjutant shouted out each man's name before throwing their letters and parcels to them.

James relaxed on his bunk to read a copy of a newspaper his step-father Papa Jon had phoned to say was on its way and also to tell James that the article was about how James's real father had died. James had felt nothing after the phone call about his father but was interested in what the newspaper article said and read it through carefully:

26th June 2020

"It was reported today at the London Coroner's office that the recent demise of one Raymond Alan Henderson had been discussed extensively. Henderson's body was found at the bottom of a wishing well after the owner of an Alsatian dog was alerted by its loud barking. Upon investigating, the owner of the dog looked down into the well and saw the shape of a man's body. He called the police and the body was removed. The autopsy revealed that both legs were broken and the man died of starvation. The death was investigated for suicide as the police said that the dead man's building company had been declared bankrupt when a major building company listed on the FT 1000 kept undercutting his prices on job tenders and Henderson's company was unable to carry on trading. The doctor conducting the autopsy could not give a clear time of death as there was a stream at the bottom of the well where fresh water could have been drunk and, unusually, during the autopsy, it was revealed that there traces of banana skins still left in the man's stomach. He could not tell how long the man had lived with the agony of two broken legs and also the secure knowledge he was completely unable to climb out of the well just using his hands and arms. The case was adjourned when the Judge declared that the death of Raymond Alan Henderson was accidental."

James, lying on his bunk bed, clenched his fist in the air and only said one word after reading the final judgement…. "Yes!"

It was the easiest thing in the world for Papa Jon to bankrupt his father's building companies. Jon just undercut everything Ray bid for and, in the end, there was no more work for him.

It was even easier for James to 'accidentally' bump into Ray again in a pub, buy him a few drinks for his life-saving shout "Look out below!," slip him a 'Mickey Finn' and when Ray went to the toilet, deliver a well-trained chop just below his right ear to render him unconscious. Only thirty minutes later, James had driven Ray to the secluded spot where the disused well was. He derived a great deal of satisfaction from dropping his father in legs first to hear the sound of broken bones on contact at the end of the fall. This would ensure he wouldn't be able to climb out, rain or no rain.

James wanted his father to suffer more than the average six weeks where people could survive on water, so he threw down a bunch of bananas for him to eat. When he threw them down the well, he shouted out "Look out below!"

The Final Tour

Shirley Anne Vaughn, or 'Ms. Vaughn' as she liked to be called, was standing in the middle of the stage, behind the curtains of the Spa Pavilion Theatre in the seaside town of Felixstowe. She waited with baited breath for the backstage announcement "We have 'Front of House' clearance." This meant the show's compere, Ms. Vaughn's manager, Harvey Johnson, would be introducing the show, the curtains would be opening, and the band would be playing her introduction music.

She would go straight into a medley of four of the greatest hits of the Sixties sung by the famous stars of the day, Dusty Springfield, Helen Shapiro, Lulu and Sandy Shaw. When she said 'the band', she was actually only working with a three-piece piano player, drummer and bass player. All three were playing along to pre-recorded tracks Harvey had paid for at a local studio out of his own pocket. Harvey was promoting the show and everything had to be kept to a tight budget.

Shirley loved theatre work. Obviously T.V. was the highest profile but, to be honest, two hours in make-up just to talk to a couple of youngster on breakfast television didn't quite do it for Shirley. It was the 'Roar of the Paint and the Smell of the Crowd' as the old variety acts used to say. She wasn't a big lover of gigging the clubs either. If she had to choose, it had to be theatre work she loved the most. The audience weren't standing at a bar ignoring her act, they weren't engaged in conversation with friends, they had paid their ticket money and sat, expectantly, waiting for you to entertain them. When she did perform well, and in the old days the response to a number one act was phenomenal, the applause at the end of each song was like a warm shower reaching and tingling every part of her body. She couldn't wait to get started.

The curtains opened and Harvey's voice echoed through the house P.A. system, "Ladies and Gentlemen, the one and only Miss Shirley Anne Vaughn!"

There was a smattering round of applause. A five hundred seater, the Spa Pavilion was to be the first gig of her final tour. Trouble was the theatre had only sold thirty-eight tickets. Harvey managed to boost the numbers by comping half of the holidaymakers in Felixstowe that afternoon. The first two rows were full and, because of the strong spotlights, Shirley could only see these and therefore assumed the rest of the theatre was full.

She belted the medley out, her voice not as strong as when she was a one-hit wonder in the sixties with 'Charlie's Girl', but everyone likes a trier and the audience gave her a polite response.

Shirley liked to drop a few 'names' during her act. "I'd to carry on with a song I performed on the 'Wogan' show." The fact that dear old Terry had been dead for ten years didn't have the response she was hoping for. If she said she worked with Peter

Kay or Michael McIntyre, it might have had the desired effect. The fact was Shirley hadn't changed her act in years. She was a good enough singer to cover an Adele song or even Susan Boyle at a push but no, her act, and her life, was firmly stuck in the sixties.

Harvey had been her manager ever since he discovered her singing for a dance band at the local Lorcano ballroom. He had been asked to find a decent singer to demo a new song which had just been written called 'Charlie's Girl'.

Shirley was excited to go into a recording studio for the first time and gave it all of her youthful enthusiasm. The song was originally intended for Sandy Shaw but when Sandy's management heard it, they decided it wasn't quite right for Sandy's more jazz influenced style. The record company, obviously a bit miffed at this and the fact that they'd already paid out in studio time, decided to release it anyway with little hope of it being a hit. Luckily enough, a Radio 1 DJ's wife had just given birth to a little girl who they named 'Charlie' and he played it non-stop. It zoomed up the charts and incredibly, hit the number one spot for two weeks, only to be knocked off by a Benny Hill comedy song.

Harvey was dreading the first-half interval when Shirley would leave the stage waving at the audience. She was bound to notice, without the glare of the follow spots, that the theatre was practically empty.

Sure enough when Harvey went into Shirley's dressing room, she turned on him.

"What's going on? Why is there no one here to see me? My last tour was a sell-out."

"Your last tour was forty years ago," replied Harvey."

"You couldn't have advertised it enough," said Shirley accusingly.

Harvey thought back to the many hours spent with his younger sister Louise working on her computer and she knew all about Facebook and Instagram. He had spent hundreds of pounds on Googles ads. He also paid for a half page spread in the Stage magazine announcing her Final Tour. He even got her a spot on Breakfast TV for God's sake.

"I can't think of any other way of telling the world about your tour. It's been on local radio all week. There's posters everywhere, there's even a banner on the first main roundabout when you enter the town. I cannot think of anything else I can do. I have spent a lot of money backing this tour." Harvey was getting really annoyed.

"Well, I've got to back on and entertain what few fans I have left. You better think of something to get the next gig busy or I'll just refuse to go on."

Harvey knew this would never happen. Shirley was right. The tour needed something that would become headline news.

The next gig at the Wyvern Theatre in Swindon the following week was a little bit better attended as Harvey had booked a popular local group to open the first half. Now Shirley was only doing the second half, she could condense her act to singing all of her best songs including, of course, 'Charlie's Girl'. It made for a better show. Most of the audience stayed for the second half. Harvey persuaded Shirley to change a few things.

"Instead of saying the next song was recorded by The Shirelles, say it was actually covered by Amy Winehouse and this is her version of 'Will You Still Love Me Tomorrow'. Instead of saying this next song was written by Bob Dylan, just say you are now going to sing Adele's 'Make you Feel My Love'. The audience will think you are more current and up-to-date on what's happening in today's music scene."

So for the next few gigs, Harvey booked a popular local act and Shirley closed the show. It was a better format but the audience numbers were still down. Harvey, as the promoter, was losing a lot of money. He had to pay a five hundred pounds deposit to secure the bookings on twelve theatres and the deal was a 70/30 split. This was a great deal if he could fill the venue, as Harvey would get 70% of the total gross, with a possible gross pay out of seven thousand pounds if he could fill it.

Harvey had booked only the 500 seater theatres as they were cheaper but they had to do better business to stop Harvey going bankrupt. He had thought of selling his 1965 Rolls Royce Silver Shadow to fund the tour but Shirley just screamed at him.

"What the effing hell am I going to turn up in at the theatres stage door, an effing Uber?"

The stage door of theatres was usually at the back of the theatres next to where the roadies would bring the equipment directly onto the back of the stage. There was a doorway usually guarded by a security man to stop the public from gaining entrance into the theatre. This didn't stop the fans from queuing up at the stage door waiting for the 'Stars' to arrive so they could ask for autographs or get them to sign old records or L.P.'s as they were called back in the day. They would wait before the show and then rush around to the back of the theatre to catch a glimpse of the 'Stars' leaving after the show.

Needless to say, there was only one or two waiting to meet Shirley on arrival. She loved it, signing autographs and talking to her fans. One of the few regulars turning up at the gigs was a real awkward goofy looking fella. It was him who gave Harvey an idea. He would leak to the press that he was having to put extra security at Shirley's gigs as she was being stalked by an overzealous fan. The story was he had even turned up her house and had to be forcibly removed. With the help of his sister, Louise, they put out 'Fake News' on various social media channels about how Shirley was in constant danger but decided to carry on with the tour.

The numbers attending the shows increased and now Shirley was performing to a decent crowd of about 200 at every gig.

Harvey was pleased as he was nearly breaking even now. When the police interviewed Harvey about the stalker, Harvey gave them an accurate description of the goofy fan who turned up at every gig. The poor sod was arrested on suspicion and released with a warning not to go within 500 yards of Shirley's home or any of her shows. The arrest even made Sky News. The beauty of it all was even Shirley believed it all. Harvey hadn't mentioned a word about his scheme to anyone other than his sister. They could see no harm in it. That was until the very last gig. It was at the Core Theatre Corby when all hell broke loose.

Shirley had a habit of just wearing a flimsy bathrobe whilst waiting to go on. She got the idea when she got told that was what Sir John Gielgud wore whilst he was getting ready. She would sit and do her make-up and hair, and a few minutes before she got the 'Five minutes, Ms Vaughn' call, she would slide into her tight-fitting dress, put on her six-inch stilettos, stand up to check herself in the full-length mirror and make her way to the side of the stage to wait for front of house clearance. It was the busiest show out of the twelve and Harvey was well-pleased his little scheme got the publicity the tour needed.

Shirley was sitting doing her make-up when all of the sudden, the goofy geek burst into the room proclaiming his innocence. He said he would never harm her and he had never ever been near her home. Shirley got up to shout for help. The intruder grabbed her, pleading with her to listen and, during the struggle, her bathrobe slipped off, leaving her completely naked.

"I'm sorry, I'm sorry," the poor misguided soul kept saying. He was just a sixties fan whose biggest love in life was sixties music and especially the music of Ms Shirley Vaughn. He turned to run out of the dressing room and let go of Shirley who fainted and fell to the floor. By this time, Harvey had heard the commotion and with the help of one of the stage hands, went to Shirley's dressing room. They both saw a man running out of the stage door.

"You run after him, I'll see if Ms Vaughn is OK."

Harvey was shocked to find Shirley lying naked on the dressing room floor. She had both her hands around her own throat and was choking. Her face was turning blue. It was clear she was having a heart attack. Harvey rushed from the dressing room to call for help whilst he pressed the three 9's on his mobile phone.

The paramedics were there within 15 minutes but it was too late. Ms Shirley Vaughn, sixties icon, died of a heart attack whilst fighting off an intruder just before she was due to go on stage for her final performance.

The next few days were bedlam for Harvey. Interviews with Sky News, talking to Piers Morgan on Breakfast T.V. about what Piers kept referring to as 'The Murder of an Icon.'

Telephone interviews with all of the 'Red Tops' and an invitation, when he has fully recovered from the shock of his client's death, to write his life story and that of Shirley's, with OK! Magazine. There was even mention of him appearing on the next 'I'm a Celebrity...'

The goofy geek was tried and sentenced to twelve months imprisonment, and the charge of manslaughter was dropped. He was found guilty of breaking the conditions of his restraining order by approaching Ms. Vaughn. The judge took pity on the lad and suspended the sentence for one year.

Harvey was in his office when his landline started ringing. Harvey was surprised as it was a while since anyone had phoned his business line.

"Hi Harvey, Frank Morgan from Universal Music. I need to talk to you about re-releasing Shirley's recordings in an album we'd like to call 'The Final Tour' and, obviously as you own the copyright to all her work, there would be an upfront payment followed by a lucrative royalty deal."

Several weeks later, Harvey was sitting in Shirley's house which she left him in his will, a very nice deal signed with Sky Living to talk about his life in showbiz, and news that the re-release of 'Charlie's Girl' was this week's No.1 in the music download charts.

Perhaps he wouldn't have to sell his Roller after all.

The Family Day Out

There was excitement in the air in the Williams' household.

It was young Billy's eleventh birthday and his dad, Richard, had planned a big surprise. Billy had no idea what his mum, Tracy, and dad had planned for the family day out. Billy had helped butter the sandwiches for the picnic but, as yet, he hadn't received any birthday presents.

"You'll just have to wait young man," Richard said winking across the kitchen to Tracy who just smiled and shook her head. She hadn't agreed with the birthday present, saying it was too much money for an eleven year old, but, as always, Richard gave her a hug and a nice kiss and got his own way.

Richard was a Cost and Works Accountant with Walkers, the crisp firm in Leicester, and to relieve the pressure that his work put upon him he would look forward to his passion that he could indulge in most weekends, flying his P.A.28 Cherokee light aircraft. It was his pride and joy. He kept the all-metal four-seater in its own hanger at Leicester Airport.

Although a smallish aeroplane, it looked fabulous in its blue and white livery with a 140 bhp engine fitted that could reach speeds of 150 mph. He had recently been awarded his pilot's licence and was currently training for an instrument rating so he would be able to fly in all kinds of weather.

At the moment though, it was strictly V.F.R. (Visual Flight Rules) only.

Richard often took the family to Leicester Airport to watch the aeroplanes and helicopters come and go. Although the runways were concrete, they weren't long enough to take holiday jets so the traffic was mostly taken up with training and pleasure flights. The aircraft tower was a relic from the Second World War with the flight training offices downstairs and the aircraft control office upstairs next to a really nice restaurant which gave a commanding view over the airfield. It was a lovely day when they had decided to take a picnic and sit in front of the control tower on the grass and enjoy the pleasure of watching the aeroplanes fly by.

"What's the runway in use today, son?" asked Richard.

Billy had always loved aeroplanes and quickly answered, "Runway 270, due west." It was a fairly easy question to answer as nine times out of ten in central England, the prevailing winds came from the west and, like birds, you always took off into the wind.

There was a trainee student doing 'circuits', taking off and turning left until he was at 1000 feet then turning downwind before turning for 'finals to land'. The aircraft would then land, throttle up, and take off again for another circuit. This was known as 'touch and go'. Billy enjoyed watching the aeroplane. It was a Cessna 170, a two-seater trainer with a tricycle undercarriage like the Cherokee, a lot easier to land than the old-fashioned tail dragger. Billy would look up at his dad when the student's attempt at landing ended up bouncing up and down the runway.

"You'll have to fly better than that if you want to join the R.A.F. son," said Robert with a smile. Billy had already put his name down to join the local branch of the Air Cadets and at the tender age of eleven, he would proudly state that after the R.A.F. had taught him to fly, he would leave and go to Dubai to work for Emirates Airline.

"Why's that, son?" asked Richard, already knowing the answer.

"Because they pay £165k a year, Dad."

Billy laughed at this as he knew it wound his mother up when he said it. She didn't want her only son to go off to Dubai, she wanted him to stay at home and get a job at nearby East Midlands Airport.

It was after the picnic that Billy was presented with his birthday gift. His Mum handed him a large box wrapped up in fancy wrapping paper and together both parents said, "Happy Birthday Son."

Billy feverishly tore open the wrapping paper to discover the box contained something he had only dreamt of in his wildest dreams. It was a Flight Simulator set-up, with joysticks, throttles for any choice of engines, and two-foot rudders to help fly the aeroplanes on Billy's computer screen at home.

Billy had wondered why his dad bought some extra memory for his Apple Mac computer saying that he might need it for his homework at his new senior school next term. It would now be perfect to power the flight simulator.

He could learn to fly anything from a Spitfire to a Boeing 737. Billy could not wait to get it home, wire it up, and fly off to Hong Kong from Gatwick airport. He jumped up and gave both his parents a massive hug saying "Thank You" over and over again.

"And there's more!" said Richard.

Billy repeated what his dad had just said, "More?"

"You know Dan, my flight instructor. I've had a word with him. We're all going flying today and Dan is going to let you sit in the pilot's seat and, when we are cruising at 2000 feet, he will hand control over to you to fly straight and level for a bit. He may even let you do a couple of turns."

Billy couldn't contain his excitement.

Twenty minutes later, Dan came over to join them. "Are you all ready to go flying?"

There was an enthusiastic response from everyone. Dan had already done the external checks on the Cherokee. He had checked the aileron and rudder movements and when he had everyone onboard safely seated with their harness tight and secure, he started preparations to call the tower for start-up and taxi clearance to runway 270. He had issued everyone with headphones so they could listen to the radio.

Just before he called the tower to seek permission to start-up and taxi to runway 270, Richard, who was in the rear seat behind the pilot, noticed Dan's seat belt harness wasn't as tight as it should be.

"No problems, Richard," said Dan.

"I like to be able to move about when I'm instructing."

"Leicester Tower, this is Golf Oscar Bravo India Pappa requesting start-up and taxi clearance for runway 270." Dan's voice was clear and precise.

"India Pappa, this is Leicester Tower, you have clearance to start-up and taxi to runway 270. The wind is currently due west at 15 knots."

After Dan had started the engine using the electronic starter, and whilst they were taxiing, Dan let Billy operate the throttle and was impressed at how smooth the movements were. He let Billy think he was steering the aeroplane, but it was Dan who was doing the rudder control using the dual controls all trainer aeroplanes were fitted with.

When they reached the edge of the taxiing area, Dan brought the aircraft directly into wind and to a full stop. "We're going to do a magneto check to see if the electrics are working. Billy, I need you to open your side skylight window and shout "Clear Prop" at the top of your voice. This is just in case anyone is near to the propeller when we bring it to full power, OK?"

Billy opened the side skylight window. "Clear Prop!" he shouted.

"And again, this time louder," said Dan.

"Clear Prop!!!" shouted the young lad with bags of enthusiasm.

Dan was practically standing on the brakes as he increased the engine to full power momentarily to check both magnetos that provide the spark for the cylinder heads to fire. Both magnetos were working satisfactorily. Dan brought the engine revs back down to idle. Dan explained that every light aircraft had two magnetos in case, during a flight, one failed.

Billy was taking all of this in. He was learning all the time.

"Leicester Tower, India Oscar requesting permission to take off," said Dan.

"India Papa, you are clear for runway 270, no known conflicting traffic."

Dan asked Billy to look around to see if there was any other aircraft in the circuit and, when he himself had checked, he entered the runway.

"Everyone set?" asked Dan. All three passengers nodded their heads.

"OK Billy, follow me through on the controls."

Billy put his hand on the throttle and gradually increased power until, when they had reached the speed of 70 knots, Dan, with Billy's help, gradually pulled back on the joystick, and with the help of both feet, keeping the rudders straight. The P.A.28 started to climb at a steady 500 feet per minute.

The flight lasted about thirty minutes an Dan let Billy temporarily take the controls to keep the aeroplane straight and level and even let him do a couple of climbing turns. All the while, Richard and Tracy were sitting proud as punch enjoying the spectacular scenery of the English countryside from 5000 feet.

"OK Billy, let's get back and let your dad have a go at some instrument flying. Do you and your mum want to come with us?"

Tracy looked at young Billy's pleading face and agreed. Billy let out a "Yes!" and gave his mum a fist pump.

Dan performed a perfect three point landing, with the nose wheel touching down exactly the same time as the two main wheels under the wings. Once again, he let Billy taxi back where they swopped seats. Billy sat in the back with his mum as Richard was now in the pilot's seat ready for instruction in how to fly an aircraft in cloud, bad weather, and eventually qualify to fly at night.

The atmosphere was a little more serious when Richard took controls and, even though he had passed his test, Dan was critical of his flying ability. "When you have to climb to 500 feet, it means 500 feet. You're climbing at 400 feet. If you start the circuit wrong, you will never achieve an accurate finals to land."

Richard nodded and concentrated even harder.

"Richard, the circuit height's not 1200, feet its 1000 feet."

Richard adjusted the power downwards slightly causing the aeroplane to drop the necessary 200 feet.

It was clear Richard was not having a particularly good day. He knew he would have to be on the ball when they entered the cloud base currently at 6000 feet.

The instruments required were speed, steady at 100mph, compass and gyro, steady at 270 degrees. The pitch control instrument, which is just a picture of a small aeroplane, was used to ensure the aircraft was flying straight and level at all times. The ball and slip indicator, if flown correctly, would ensure accurate turning.

Richard started to do better. Dan made only one comment when they were turning." Now, now, not too steep, you'll stall the engine and we'll go into a spin and we don't want that now, do we?"

Richard nodded and corrected the turn. It was difficult for most pilots to fly an aeroplane without reference to the horizon. Sometimes you feel as though you are climbing even though the pitch control says you are not. Then when you're turning, the slip and ball indicator says you've got it spot on.

"Trust your instruments at all times. It's only your own sense of balance playing tricks on you," Dan advised.

In the rear seats, this was not what Tracy and Billy were looking forward to. The atmosphere was not fun and enjoyable; it was rather tense and, to be honest, a little bit scary as all around them was just solid cloud and they were beginning to feel a little bit claustrophobic.

"Right, that's enough for today. You'll be getting tired, takes us down to 2000 feet and aim for overhead at Leicester Airport." Dan relaxed back into his seat.

That's when it happened....

Richard took hold of the throttle to bring the revs down from the cruising rate of 2000 R.P.M. to 1500 R.P.M. so he could place the aircraft into a gentle descent down to 5000 feet and clear the cloud base. As he was carefully bringing the throttle down, he distinctly felt a shudder in the cable that shouldn't have been there.

"Dan, I think we've got a problem with the throttle cable...."

"What do you mean, problem?" replied Dan.

"I think it's broken!"

"It can't be, here, let me take a look." Dan grabbed the throttle with his left hand and, for some reason only known to him, he raised the throttle to it's full on position, raising the level of revs to their maximum of 2500 R.P.M. "Feels OK to me." Dan's tone was more hopeful than positive.

It was only when he let go did they both see the throttle drop quickly to the bottom of its 'off' position with no change in the revs. They were now flying at maximum engine power with no control over the engine. The aircraft immediately started to climb.

"Damn, what do we do now!?" asked Richard.

Dan was already on the radio. "Mayday! Mayday! This is Golf Oscar Bravo India Pappa with four people on board. We are flying at full power with a faulty throttle cable. Can you advise?"

Dan was struggling with the controls. He was having to use all his strength to keep the nose down to stop the aeroplane from climbing.

They broke clear of the cloud base and Dan levelled off at 5000 feet to wait for instructions.

"India Pappa, what is your estimated position, course direction and height, over?"

"Leicester Tower, we are flying due east, ten miles from the airfield at 5000 feet." Dan had taken over radio contact to allow Richard to use all of his concentration to fly the aeroplane.

"India Pappa, you are going to have to do a forced landing. Approach the runway at approximately 50 feet and cut the engine to zero power and glide the aeroplane onto the runway, do you copy?"

Dan stated the aeroplanes call sign as the recognised term of agreement "India Pappa."

"India Pappa, I understand you are now flying at your maximum speed of 150mph, am I correct?"

"India Pappa."

"India Pappa, the runway at Leicester is too short for an aircraft landing at your velocity. We need to guide you to a military base where the runways are much longer. You need to turn 180 degrees. You will soon see the town of Stamford on your nose. R.A.F. Wittering is beyond the town next to the A1 so you should spot it easily. We will have full accident response vehicles following you down the runway which is over a mile long. It should be enough."

"I bet the ambulances and fire engines can't do 150 mph though," remarked Richard.

"That's not helping, Richard." Dan glanced behind to see the worried look on Tracy's face as she was hugging Billy and covering his face. He was no longer a future pilot, just a scared young boy in his mother's arms.

"Right Richard, that's the plan. You are pilot in command so it's your job to land the aeroplane whilst it's my job to cut the engine as soon as we see the large white numbers denoting 270 on the runway. The aircraft will kick violently to the right. You must be ready to kick in left rudder to stay straight and level. Then you will have to glide the aeroplane down onto the runway. You got that?"

"Clear as mud," said Richard who was now hunched over the controls concentrating for all of his dear life and the life of his family.

Richard got the aeroplane down to 500 feet as he flew over Stamford, narrowly avoiding the church spire that stood proudly in the centre of town. The residents were used to low flying military aircraft from the nearby base but not single engine jobs. Military could fly at any height, anywhere;

light aircraft had to be at least 1500 feet above buildings and population. So a few of the more knowledgable residents gazed up and were puzzled as the sound of the screaming engine filled the sky.

"There's the runway, dead ahead," said Dan.

There was an ambulance to the left of the runway with two fire engines ready to give chase at the right of the runway.

"Once I cut the power above the numbers, be ready for that violent kick to the right."

"Let's hope the runway's long enough," replied Richard. He had to fly at 150mph at only 50 feet above the ground, something neither of the pilots had done before. The tension in the cockpit was acute. The sound of sobbing from behind of a frightened young boy only added to Richard's determination to bring the aeroplane down safely.

He was now low enough to be skimming over houses at Burghley House, north of Stamford. As they raced passed the emergency vehicles, they flew over the large white numbers. Dan leaned forward and switched both magnetos off, killing the engine stone dead.

The aeroplane lurched to the right but Richard managed to catch it with his left rudder which he used, along with the right one, to fly the aeroplane straight and level.

They were gliding at 150mph and Richard could see the emergency vehicles tearing along the runway to try and catch up to them. Richard could see the end of the runway fast approaching.

"Put us down on the ground for heaven's sake!!" Dan screamed.

Richard panicked and reacted to the shout by pushing the joystick forward too forcibly. The aircraft bounced like a balloon. Richard thought momentarily of the student pilot's landing a few hours ago. Once again, he made the mistake of putting the nose down too steeply. This time, the aircraft didn't bounce. The nose wheel was not built to take the force of a high-speed landing. The aircraft collapsed onto the runway, the screeching of metal gouging into concrete mixed with the screaming of the rear seat passengers filled the air.

The propeller, though the engine was switched off, was still turning at a high rate of knots. When the propeller hit the concrete, followed by a large scraping noise, it catapulted the machine into the air. The aircraft made its last fateful three second flight and then crashed to the ground with sparks flying. Both wings were full of petrol but it was the left wing that was mangled and leaking fuel.

Richard quickly undid his harness. Dan was unconscious with his head on the dashboard and was bleeding heavily.

"Get out, you two!" Richard turned and screamed at Tracy and Billy. "Hurry, there's fuel leaking!"

AS Richard ran around the damaged left wing, the fuel ignited. He stopped and stared at the licking flames, and self-preservation kicked in. He turned and ran. As he did, the left wing exploded, throwing

Richard onto the grass verge beside the runway. He didn't know if he had been knocked unconscious or just dazed, but he managed to stand up screaming "Tracy! Billy! Tracy!! Billy!!"

He ran around the wreckage only to see both of them safely in the arms of a large fireman.

"Stand back, the right wing might explode as well!" the fireman shouted to Richard.

Paramedics from the ambulance were hurrying to the scene and the second fire engine was already unravelling their hose ready to dowse the aircraft with foam.

"What about Dan?" Richard could clearly see Dan's body still prostrate on the dashboard. With no concern for his own safety, he climbed onto the wing, opened the door, all the time cursing Dan for having loose safety restraints that enabled his body to crash into the dashboard.

He undid the culprits and with the aid of the fireman who had now bravely followed him onto the plane, they were both able to drag Dan's inert body to safety.

The paramedics, seeing there were casualties, went back for a stretcher. Meanwhile, the second fire crew was successfully dowsing the stricken aeroplane. The aircraft wreckage was completely covered in foam. As a result, there was no second explosion from the right-hand wing.

Richard hugged his wife and son. He turned to look at the charred wreck. He felt no passion for flying now.

The ambulance took them to Leicester General Accident & Emergency. They radioed ahead to let them know one passenger was critical and the other three needed to be treated for shock, and in Richard's case, a few burns and bruises.

It was a few weeks later when Richard was visiting a heavily bandaged Dan that, when asked if he ever would fly again, Richard shook his head and quickly changed the subject.

The Williams family would have many more days out, but none at Leicester Airport. The box containing the flight simulator controls was sent back unopened and Billy never did join the Air Cadets. When the insurance money came through from the accident, Richard didn't even consider buying a new aeroplane. Tracy and Richard decided to build a new conservatory onto the back of their house instead.

That fateful flying family day was never ever mentioned again.

Can You Tempt A Saint?

Rory McIntosh was only fifteen years old when he started working at the Corby branch of ASDA. With no qualifications from school, he had, however, a great work ethic. He had two paper rounds every morning and a part-time job on a Saturday at the local 24-hour McDonalds. Unfortunately, the school he went to mistakenly thought he was an academic. Physics, French, Latin meant nothing to Rory. If asked, he could reel off the lyrics to the first Coldplay album but no one ever asked him.

Rory was chuffed he had passed the interview and was now stacking shelves wearing the green company polo shirt with the word ASDA emblazoned on the back with the strapline "We are happy to help" written below the company logo. Rory only knew one thing in life. If you worked hard all week then on a Friday someone would give you a wage packet full of money.

Rory enjoyed his job. He especially enjoyed helping the customers with their constant enquiries. When asked where the Manuka honey was instead of ASDA's own brand, he didn't just say "Aisle 27, left-hand side, halfway down." Rory would stop what he was doing and take the customer to where the product was. He liked to chat with the customers and was a big fan of the American way of finishing contact with a customer with the inevitable "Have a nice day."

Rory never rushed off to the staffroom to check his smart phone on his break. He always finished whatever job he was doing, have a quick cup of tea, and then get back to work.

It was only his second day at work when he spotted his first shoplifter.

It was a young mum who casually slipped a bottle of vodka and hid it in the folds on the hood of the pram she was pushing. Rory followed her to the counter and accused her of stealing vodka. The young girl vehemently denied it and when Rory retrieved the bottle from the hood of the pram, she just walked off out of the store.

"Don't worry lad, she'll just go off to Tesco's to try the same scam." Betty, the cashier, had been at ASDA for over ten years and was immune to it all.

Rory was really annoyed. What if the girl had got away with it? The next stock take would prove sales of vodka were down and who were the natural suspects? The shelf stackers, that's who. Rory was determined he was not going to lose his job because of shoplifters. The next time he caught a young lad stealing an expensive games console, he apprehended him and marched him off to the security office.

It soon came to the management's attention that there was a young lad working in the store, never late, always wearing a collar and tie, with a great work ethic who was better at catching shoplifters than the security men who seemed to spend more time in their office than on the shop floor.

Rory was over the moon to be offered the chance to go on a junior management course. It meant going to college part-time to get some business qualifications. He discovered he was good at statistics, commerce and accounting. If it had anything to do with business, Rory was interested and within six months, he passed his exams and was promoted to Junior Manager.

It never seemed to amaze Rory what people would do to try and steal stuff. Stolen goods stuffed up jumpers. Frozen chickens down trousers. The classic one was when Rory stopped a young lad dressed in overalls wheeling the fruit machine out of the cafe bar telling Rory he was from the fruit machine company and he had been called out to collect it for repair. Rory laughed as he was the one who made phone calls to companies about repairs. He could not help cracking up when he looked outside to see the young lad's accomplice waiting to help lift the machine into a waiting Black Cab taxi to make their get-away.

As both teenagers were known to the police, after Rory gave them an accurate description, they were arrested and ended up doing 100 hours community service.

After a year of exemplary service, Rory was offered his own store in the nearby town of Kettering. The store was brand new and it was Rory's job to interview and train the prospective employees. He was soon able to sort the wheat from the chaff. He never liked being in his office for too long. He liked to be on the shop floor supervising the staff, chatting to the customers and doing his favourite thing, catching shoplifters. He couldn't understand why people still chanced their luck at stealing when it was known throughout the store that the new manager's forte was catching thieves and, more importantly, getting them arrested.

One day, Rory was called into the office with a further job promotion by a visiting Director of the company.

"Rory, how would like to move to London, Enfield in fact?" We're having a new store built there and we want you to manage it."

Rory was obviously delighted said he would be keen to get started.

"There's a ten percent increase in your salary with a better company car, a Jaguar instead of a Mondeo. Sound OK?"

The Director then stood, walked round the perimeter of Rory's office, before continuing. "Rory, it is well-known that you have an eye for a thief but have you an eye for a fiddle? I need you to investigate a store in Manchester. Not a full-size store, just an ASDA Express based inside a filling station off the M62. We've compared takings with other similar-sized operations and it is not doing the trade it should be. I would like you to go there, with the company stocktaker, when he is doing his next stock check, under the guise of being a trainee to see if you can sniff out what the problem is."

Rory said he was up for a challenge and ten days later, found himself travelling to Manchester with the Company Stocktaker.

In conversation with the stocktaker on the journey, they agreed there were three main ways of fiddling. Stealing stock from the stock cupboards or cellars where the beer, wines and spirits are stored. This is where a good manager is worth his salt. He will check every item down to the last bottle to ensure what he has ordered is what is delivered. Don't give the delivery men an inch or they will definitely take a mile.

The second main way to lose stock is by the staff taking liberties. They agreed it is a well-known statistic that one in ten members of staff actively steal from the job they work in. This is why most small businesses will only employ family and even then, it can all go pear-shaped.

But the main way there is problems with theft in a managed business is the manager stealing from the coffers. If the manager is clever, he will find a way to hide the fraud. If he is skimming from the top, he will use some of the stolen cash to buy stock to put back onto the shelves. This keeps the stock result as it should be but obviously decimates the takings. They agreed this was the most likely scenario in Manchester.

The manager met them cordially, and gave them a cup of tea and sandwich as they must be hungry after the long journey north. He joined them going round all the shelves, helping with the count. He also showed them the cellar where the wines and spirits were stored and, once again, with his help, made sure the count was accurate.

He then went off to get the paperwork that the stocktaker needed to check - invoices, delivery notes etc. Stocktaking even at a small ASDA Express store took all day to do all the calculations. Basically, the value of last month's stock was taken away to give a stock valuation figure sold. This figure should accurately match the takings that had been banked in the last month. The stocktaker's portable stock computer printed out the figures that showed everything balanced as it should, allowing the stocktaker to give a copy to the manager with the comments that both sets of figures matched each other and, and as far as he could make out, there were no stock problems.

On the way out of the store, after a very long day, Rory turned around to the manager and said, "Pardon my ignorance, as I am only a trainee, but I have been to several stores now and yours doesn't seem to be as busy as the others. I spoke to the manager of the petrol station and his comments were that business had never been so good."

The manager delayed his response as he was obviously annoyed what Rory was inferring. "I have lost a lot of my customers to the new Morrisons built two miles down the road. People will travel anywhere to get a can of beans five pence cheaper."

Rory said his farewell and asked the stocktaker to take him to a hotel and could he borrow the companies' master key for the store.

Rory waited till after the store, and the petrol station, had closed for the day before making his way back to the store.

He had that old familiar gut feeling about the manager. Everything was too perfect today. Rory was sure he was on the take, but how?

Using the companies keys and inputting the alarm code, Rory spent the next hour fitting small digital wi-fi cameras discreetly hidden in the ceiling lights, each one pointing at the tills. Rory was convinced this was where the money was going missing.

He spent the next day at his hotel staring at the split screen images on his iPad from the four cameras pointing at four tills. After two hours, his neck was stiff and his back was aching and he was thinking about taking a break when a customer who had come in the store shortly after it opened came in again. She asked once again for a pack of cigarettes and if she could have 'cash back'. Twice in one morning, she needed 'cash back'?

Rory rewound the computer. The company policy on 'cash back' was a maximum of thirty pounds. Rory cursed the camera hadn't picked up the transaction. He rewound the video back to the start and there she was, the same mature middle-aged lady asking for cigarettes and 'cash back.'

There it was clearly in black and white. Not three ten pound notes but three twenty pound notes. "Gotcha!" said Rory.

The next morning it was a pleasure to see the shock on the manager's face when Rory walked in and identified who he really was and what he had been tasked to do by the Director. "Can we go through to your office, please," Rory asked.

Rory sat opposite the manager and had a real stroke of luck. There was a framed picture on the manager's desk of the manager and, supposedly, his wife. In fact, it was the same middle-aged woman who was receiving double what she should have received in "cash back".

The manager's face went white as Rory explained his findings.

"What's the name of the member of staff who gives out the sixty pounds instead of thirty each time? She worked on till number four yesterday."

"That's my daughter," the manager replied, near to tears.

"Only one other thing. The tills are all linked to the company's mainframe computer. Why didn't the print out at the end of the day show sixty pounds instead of thirty?"

"My son's at University studying Computer Studies. He was able to log into till number four and change the software so when the cash back button was pressed, it would print out thirty pounds."

At the court case where the whole family was charged with fraud, they admitted taking £120 pounds a day every day. Approximately four thousand pounds a year for the last five years. The judge found them all guilty of fraud and theft. He sentenced the manager to a year's imprisonment with suspended sentences for his wife and two children. The judge was also nonplussed when the defence lawyer stated that his clients had not kept all the money they had stolen, as they had to buy discounted stock every week to put back into the store to keep the stocktaker happy whenever they knew he was visiting soon!

The Director took on Rory's suggestion that managers should *not* be notified when they are getting stock checked. Under the current system, crooked managers had a few days to sort out any cash discrepancies, usually borrowing from other stores on the pretext of needing change for the tills, so if there was a 'walk in' stock check, they would not be caught red-handed if stock, and cash, wasn't accounted for.

The Director put Rory's suggestion before the board and it was approved as company policy.

It was another result for Rory which got him another promotion to senior manager with a really nice Mercedes thrown in.

Rory was still waiting to take up his position at the new store at Enfield. The builders were taking forever and the grand opening promotions were cancelled twice and were just kept on hold.

"Next time you build a store, let me project manage the build. I know I can do a better job than the current guy. It should never have been agreed to pay him monthly. If he was doing it for a price, I bet you a penny to a pound that store would be open now." The Director who Rory was having lunch with nodded his head in agreement.

"I'll bear you in mind if we have another new store built. But as you know, and by saying this he was confirming rumours that had been going round ASDA for weeks, Walmart, in America, are taking us over so expect changes and hopefully further expansion. The Aldi and Lidl supermarkets of this world are killing us at the moment."

Rory also made a suggestion about altering the position of the tills. "Under the present system, customers walk in the store and buy a few items, go to the self-serve area before till number one and are out of the store in a few minutes. If you move the self-serve to the other end just pass till number twenty, the customer has to walk through the full store with a greater opportunity to impulse buy."

All the directors thought this was a great idea and would be implemented in the next new-build.

It was a few days later that, once again, Rory was asked to do another bit of investigating. His old store at Corby was seeing discrepancies in sales, in particular wines and spirits.

"We're in luck," said the Operations Director. "The Corby manager is going on holiday for a couple of weeks so it will appear natural that, as you're still waiting for Enfield to open, you can do the job of Relief Manager."

"No problem," said Rory. "I always look forward to the challenge. My experience has taught me that although you have to look out for that one staff member in ten who is actively stealing from the company, if presented with a cast iron fiddle, even the most honest of staff will join in. After all, the average ASDA store takes in over £1 million pounds a week so who's going to miss a few bottles of vodka?"

Rory enjoyed his time back in Corby. He knew the staff well and was always glad to stop and chat with regular customers. The office secretary told him, in confidence, that the existing manager spends most of his time in the office playing computer games. "Hardly ever goes out to the shop floor to supervise." Ah well! When the cat's away, the mice will play. *Not on my shift,* thought Rory.

He spent several hours looking over the accounts to get a feel for what was missing and found that the largest discrepancy was the daily sales of vodka. Walking around the store, he was sure it was not the staff. Most had worked there, like he had, from the day the store had opened and would not risk their livelihood for a few bottles of plonk. For the amount of vodka that was being stolen, the thief must be an alcoholic. Looking at the staff rotas, he noticed one thing had changed. The store was employing a new agency to provide cleaning staff. There were six staff a day working from 5am to 8am. As Rory did not start work until 9am, he had never met them. Tomorrow morning, that would all change with an 'on the spot' bag inspection.

The cleaners were quite taken aback when requested to show their bags for inspection. Rory said it was a change of company policy. The only thing that jarred with Rory's gut instinct was all the cleaners brought a litre of water to work. When asked about this, the reply was that cleaning was hard work and he should try it someday. That's what Rory hated about agency workers, you never got the same respect.

He stopped them at 8am when they were on the way out and called them in, one-by-one, for a bag check. He asked an assistant manager to supervise the other cleaners so they did not leave or go to the toilet.

Sure enough, every litre bottle of water had been poured away and filled with vodka. When threatened by the police, the head cleaner admitted they had a deal with the landlord of the nearest pub, The Nags Head, who was paying them £5 a bottle and pouring their vodka into his own empty three litre bottles and putting it up on the optic where his £5 investment would return him 32 x £3 a shot, making him a cool profit of £91 per bottle per cleaner per day. Once again Rory had cracked it. His boss was going to be well pleased.

Time went on for Rory. He had even met a nice young girl called Lucy who he had recently got married to on the understanding that ASDA came before anything else.

The Kettering store was the flagship of the company and Rory was invited down to London to meet the directors of Walmart who had come across from the States to discuss worldwide strategy for the brand and introduce 'roll back' pricing promotions to combat the opposition.

He was asked if the opportunity arose, would he project manage any new-builds in America for Walmart. It would mean moving over there to live.

Rory didn't have to think twice and several weeks later after the successful launch of the new Enfield store, Rory was asked how he felt about moving to Minnesota. Two weeks later, Rory and Lucy were on the plane, passports and visas in hand.

Rowdy Stone, who unfortunately did not look as cool as his name, sat in his office in downtown Minneapolis. He was 64 years old, looked older, and desperately wanted to join his daughter and grandchildren in Florida when he retired. The legend on the glass of his office front door read: "Rowdy Stone: Private Investigator."

His leather chair had to be as big as it was due to Rowdy's huge frame and his six-foot height. He badly needed a haircut, his moustache a trim, and a new suit, collar and tie would not go amiss. He just answered a call from the local Operations Director at the nearby new Walmart store that was being built in Minnesota. He was only weeks away from retirement and Walmart wanted him to do his usual mundane job of going through hundreds of applicants and sort out the ones he thought were suitable for an interview. The decision to hire the selected few would be the new manager's job, whose profile he had in front of him.

"Rory McIntosh from Corby, Northants, England. Twenty years of experience working for ASDA/Walmart. Top class manager with excellent motivational and promotional skills whose forte was running a tight ship due to his uncanny knack of recognising shoplifters as soon as they come into his store. He had been used to investigate fiddles and several thefts from other stores with success. He was now considered to be one of Walmart top saints in the world of management. Hard working, happily married to his corporate lawyer wife, Lucy, and considerable expertise and commitment to the company by project managing the building of the new, soon to open, Walmart store in Minnesota."

Rowdy could not remember the last time he had read such nonsense. "Saint" – what is that all about? The American use of religion in every facet of their lives continued to amaze Rowdy who had seen far too much of the seedy side of life without having the need to sing "hallelujah" every morning. Mother Teresa would not be happy if she knew all you had to do to become a "Saint" nowadays was to be a top store manager! Rowdy laughed to himself.

Rowdy was about to send a report over to a client's solicitor that not only is her travelling salesman having an affair with a lady in New York, he was married to her with two kids. He enclosed the incriminating photographic evidence, a copy of the false marriage certificate, and an invoice for his bill and expenses. He no longer gave his report directly to his clients after one of them attacked him, calling him a "lousy, rotten liar". Talk about shooting the messenger.

Rowdy cast his mind back to the meeting last week when he went to the new store, which was a hive of activity, with a view to meeting the new manager to discuss how the employment laws are different in America than in England and he would be better off hiring retirees instead of young kids who would not know a hard day's work if it hit them in the face. Rory practically ignored Rowdy mumbling "thanks for all your help but, as you can see, I am very busy as I have a store to open."

Rowdy had only spent a few moments with the man but as he left the store, he had that old familiar gut feeling that Rory McIntosh was 'on the take' and Rowdy was going to make it his mission to find out how Rory intended to go about it in the new Walmart store.

The store opening was a spectacular success. Rory was featured on local television adverts and the viewers loved his English accent and beautiful English rose of a wife. The takings were as expected, the stocks were good, and the staff which Rory chose and trained were doing a great job.

In fact, it was so successful that after a couple of months, Rory and Lucy were able to move out of their rented company house and buy thir own six-bedroom villa complete with swimming pool.

Rowdy, however, knew different. He spent several weekends on surveillance watching the comings and goings at Mr. and Mrs. McIntosh's new house in a very upmarket part of the suburbs on the outside of the city. There was no way they could afford this house on a Senior Store Manger's salary. Even with bonuses, what he earned would hardly pay for the running cost of the large heart-shape swimming pool. He had to be thieving, Rowdy just knew it. But how was he going to prove it?

Rory had explained the opulence of his new houses to his bosses when he invited them to a housewarming party. Rory got a great price for their house in London where, as the house prices were extortionate and they were both very pleased with Lucy's settlement from her partnership in the top corporate lawyers firm in Manchester.

This was the one thing that made Rowdy smile the most. Apart from never having owned a house in England, Lucy did work at a corporate lawyers firm in Manchester, as a typist typing up conveyancing contracts.

Rowdy tried to think of Rory's scam from a different prospective. Rory was obviously stealing cash. Question one - how was he managing to do it? Question two - Rory also had to cover the missing cash by replacing it with stock, how was he doing that? Rowdy decided to switch tack and changed his surveillance to the actual store. The only time the store was shut was on a Sunday. Stores could open as many hours as they liked in England, but in America on a Sunday, they were restricted to the opening hours of 10am to 4pm.

Rowdy assumed any stock being delivered after hours on a Sunday would not be delivered under the full view of the front of the store, so Rowdy parked in his battered pick-up wagon a few hundred yards behind the store where he could keep an eye on any comings and goings.

Rowdy waited until 10pm and thought of turning in for the night. He was tired and hungry.

Suddenly, a set of headlights drove around the back of the store which caught his attention. It was Rory and Lucy, not in Rory's company Mercedes, that would be too obvious, but in Lucy's Cadillac DeVille. They were followed by a white van, most probably a Mercedes Sprinter. Not too big but big enough with no lettering or logos on it to stop it from being identified.

Rory approached the large metal door, pointed his car keys at it, and stood back watching the roller shutters opening upwards. The van reverse in and the door closed.

"Damn," said Rowdy, "how am I going to see inside?"

He decided he had to get closer. There were no windows or convenient doors at the rear of the building so he went around to the front. The inside of the building was in complete darkness. What were they going to do with the stock? Rowdy was peering through the front windows when the headlights of the van appeared.

"Jesus!" exclaimed Rowdy as he quickly ducked down. The driver could not have seen his bulky frame as the van drove away towards the highway. Then two strong torch lights appeared inside the store. Rowdy could not believe what he was seeing. Rory was going back in time to his first job with ASDA. He was shelf stacking! Back and forth he went from the stockroom to the appropriate shelf. It did not take long as Rory had intimate knowledge of where every stock item was to be placed. He did have a problem with a large plasma television that Lucy helped him place in the correct place in the electronics department. Rowdy took out his night time surveillance camera and clicked away merrily.

Rowdy made his way back to his truck. He had seen enough. As he drove away, part of him was pleased he had discovered how Rory was covering his tracks but why was the stock being replaced just randomly picked? That didn't sound like Rory. He was far too clever to not have every angle covered. Besides, if he had a walk-in stock in the morning, everything needed to be perfect. Accurate takings against stock sold and daily sales of every item must be close to that of all the other stores. How in the hell was he doing it?

The next day, Rowdy decided to take a trip to the Walmart store in the twin town of Minneapolis 160 miles south of Minnesota, a two and a half hour drive south of the state.

He did not want to spend any time in Rory's store as questions would be asked. Upon arrival in Minneapolis, he parked in the same size car park and went through the same front doors as his hometown store. Walking in, they had the same row of tills and then the aisles of stock. Rowdy turned left to where the cafe was, ordered a coffee, and sat where he could watch was going on.

It was a quiet Tuesday lunchtime and they only had the last six tills open 15 through to 20.

Standard procedure as till 20 was next to the self-serve area and Rowdy noticed if a customer was having a problem using the self-serve computers, it was the girl on Till 20 who left her position to help and show the customer what to do.

Rowdy could see the rationale of Rowdy's suggestion about having only the last six tills open when the store was quiet as, indeed, the customer had to walk more or less through the store to pay for their items, passing many items and promotions that encouraged impulse buying. Rowdy paid two more visits to the Minneapolis store and, satisfied he had a better feel for the operation, decided to pay a visit to Rory's store.

Rowdy was sitting in the cafe when he noticed Rory walking into the store, eyeing everything - the stock, the staff, and customers' movements. He would stop and chat to customers in a friendly manner and Rowdy wondered how he kept that charming smile looking so authentic when all the time, he was ripping off his bosses to the tune of tens of thousands of dollars.

Rowdy stationed himself next to the self-serve area. When a customer had a problem, Rory put his hand up to the girl on the last till and said, "No problem, I'll show Mrs. Green how to use the self-service till." Mrs. Green, obviously a regular to the store, laughed and valued Rory's personal touch and supreme customer service.

It was whilst Rowdy was drinking his second cup of coffee that he noticed Rory told the girl to stay on the last till several times whilst he helped self-serve customers. Why? Rory seemed obsessed with keeping the last till busy with no interruptions to the busy customer flow. It was then he noticed it. It was then everything fell into place. Rowdy kept referring to the till next to the self-serve as the 'last till', why? Because it had no number on it! IT HAD NO NUMBER! Hallelujah! The last till in every other Walmart store was till 20. In Rory's store, there was an added till, no number, Rory and Lucy's till. That's how he was getting the cash out. He project managed the building of the store. I don't suppose it took too much 'greasing of palms' with the building contractor to fit in an extra till at the end of the aisle when the store was getting built.

Rowdy now had a decision to make. He was two months from retiring, two months away from spending his last years in Florida with his daughter and grandchildren. It was then he made up his mind.

Rory was in his office early the following morning when his secretary handed him a large A3 brown envelope.

"What's this?" enquired Rory.

"I've no idea," replied the secretary. "It was hand-delivered this morning." She closed Rory's door and left him to open the envelope.

It didn't take Rory long to learn what exactly was his future was going to be. A full report of the scam, photographs of Rory and Lucy carrying in a large plasma TV, prints of the Mercedes Sprinter van and last, but not least, a picture of the last till in his store and someone had drawn an arrow towards it with the words "Shouldn't this be till 21?"

Rory must have read the report a half-dozen times. What the hell was he going to do? If his superiors found out about this, he was facing time in prison for committing serious theft and fraud.

Then his phone went.

"I will meet you in the cafe of Walmart in Minneapolis, today at noon exactly." The caller hung up. No chance to talk, no opportunity to reason. He looked at his watch. He had better leave now to make it for noon. He rushed out of the office only to return minutes later. He took a Walther PK25 revolver from his office drawer and placed it into the band of his trousers.

Rowdy smiled when Rory walked into the cafe. The look on Rory's face was a picture. "What are you doing here? I'm supposed to be meeting someone."

"You're meeting me," said Rowdy.

"You! You're only a two-bit P.I. who hasn't got two-bits to rub together."

"That may be," replied Rowdy, "but I'm the one holding the brown envelope." Rowdy took the large envelope out of his briefcase with copy of all the evidence inside and showed it to Rory.

Rory made a grab for it but Rowdy was too quick for him and pulled it back. "You think I've only got the one copy, you fool?"

Hesitating largely for effect, he then added, "Let me tell you how this is going to work out. I'm not a greedy man so every month I will invoice you for services rendered, personal protection, staff investigations and so on, and you will wire me $1k. each month to this account." He passed a bank slip with his name and account details.

"Now I know you're probably armed and you have some crazy notion of making this all go away by shooting me but in the event of an untimely demise, my solicitor has been instructed to send details of your scam to Head Office and to the police. You will then be screwed, big time. On the other hand, $1k. a month is chicken feed compared to what you're taking out of the business. Just look upon it as an insurance policy."

Rory sat with his head in his hands for what seemed an age. He thought it through. The man was right, it was not a massive amount of money to pay for Rowdy's silence and, more importantly, he would not have to tell Lucy.

"Okay, I'll agree," said Rory.

"Just one minor detail before you go," added Rowdy. "I know how you got the cash out and I know you covered it by buying in stock, but how did you know what to buy in?"

"I just took a read out of what we had sold through our own till's computer at close of play each Sunday at 4 p.m., and phoned through to our suppliers asking for a special delivery for later on that evening. I always paid the delivery men cash.

They even used to help unload the stock for us. It was perfect until you showed up."

"Actually, it was only when they started to call you a 'saint' that I began thinking no one is that perfect. In my business, I have come across professional thieves, opportunist thieves, and people, honest people, who suddenly would find them in a situation where the amount of money to be stolen would 'tempt a saint.'

Crime does pay for a certain amount of time. Rory slipped up a few years later getting too greedy by trying it all again in a new store. This time it was spotted straight away and he is doing serious time in one of the less-enamoured prisons in Minneapolis whilst Rowdy is still enjoying himself in Florida riding around in his brand new truck.

Next time you go into your local ASDA store, try counting all the tills. You never know, someone might be 'on the take'.

Love At First Sight

Roddy 'Piano Man' Richardson had never been in love. Keyboard player with well-known 1960's combo 'The Typhoons' he obviously had had, what shall we call them, 'encounters' in the night. In dressing rooms, outside dressing rooms, inside transit vans, outside... you get the picture. Definitely not a lot of love involved. You know what they say, musicians are in love firstly with themselves, then their music, and then whomever else turns up.

Roddy had never been in love. His wife Sandra was just one of several girls he was seeing on a casual basis when he was a teenager when she, unfortunately, got pregnant. In those days, you had to do the right thing and get married. The marriage had worked well, possibly due to the fact that he was always away, and his two daughters provided him with three lovely grandchildren, and they were the light of his life. But here he was, at the age of sixty-six, sitting in a cafe at Brussels railway station with pen and paper in hand trying to write to his wife to explain why he has to leave her.

Roddy left school with good qualifications in music and had been accepted at teacher training college to teach sixth formers classical piano and classical guitar. Then, out of the blue, the phone rang.

"Hey Roddy, Jack here." Jack was the lead vocalist with 'The Strong Principles', a well-known rock outfit. "You're going to love this one, buddy. We're due to go to Dubai for a three month residency and our keyboard player has let us down. Rather it's probably his wife who has let us down. What do you think, bud?"

"What do you mean 'what do I think'?"

"Roddy, it's a grand a month, everything all inclusive, and I mean *everything*. This is a great gig man. You've gotta come, you'll love it."

For some strange reason, Roddy agreed to go to Dubai before starting work at the teacher training college. The only thing he asked was "Do I have to grow my hair long and wear make-up?"

Next thing he knew, he was on a 737 to the Middle East with a bunch of guitar players who would not know a crochet from a hatchet. What had he let himself in for?

Rehearsals went well. Roddy's keyboard skills added to the band's overall sound and then it came, the first gig. Roddy was strangely nervous. He had never been nervous about anything in his life. He noticed the rest of the band got rid of their apprehensions with a couple of lines of cocaine which seemed to be readily available. Is this what they meant by 'everything'?

The gig was incredible! The hotel where their residence was pulled out all the stops with the P.A., lights and staging. Good monitors and drum riser so everyone could see 'Wacky' on the drums. I do not

130

have to tell you where he got that name from. The venue was packed, helped by a load of American sailors whose ship had docked for repairs. These boys really got into the band.

"Play some of your own stuff!" they shouted.

The band did not need to be asked twice. They went straight into a couple of original songs which went down really well.

***

The three months passed quickly. When they landed at Heathrow on their return, Roddy turned round and thanked the band for a brilliant time but he was now going to concentrate on teaching music instead of playing any more with the band.

"You'll really miss it man," was their parting words. Roddy did not realise then that they were right, he really was going to miss it.

Two months into teacher training and Roddy was bored out of his mind. He tried mixing study work during the day with playing with a covers band at night but it did not work out. It had to be one or the other.

The next phone call that made up his mind for him came from the A&R department of Universal Music. A&R stood for Artistes and Repertoire and these guys were responsible for signing new talent and deciding what material to record.

"Hi Roddy, Jack Roberts here from Universal Music. I've got a problem I'm hoping you can help me out with."

"Sure, anything I can do to help," replied Roddy.

"I've got a band in the studio. You might remember them, they're called 'The Typhoons' and they're recording their new album. I thought it would be great to record a couple of classical tracks seeing as we now have a national Classical Music channel. The trouble is our keyboard player can't play the stuff. Too many black notes apparently. I hear you're the 'go-to guy' for this sort of thing. Can you come and go through a couple of tracks with the boys?"

"Sure," said Roddy, "looking forward to it!"

So off Roddy went, down to London, with his keyboard in the boot of the car and, to cut a long story short, the manager of the band did a 'Pete Best'. He sacked the keyboard player and gave the job to Roddy.

Here he was, no longer teacher training, in a chart band which have had hits and a full diary of gigs, including in Germany and Norway, and a thousand pounds a week, plus expenses. It sure beats the hell out of a teacher's salary.

***

The years went by in a whirlwind. Roddy's superb singing added so much to the band. They did not have to rely entirely on playing instrumentals all of the time. As a result, they got a better class of gig. They were offered cruise work on the Queen Mary, headlined a Sixties Show at the London Palladium, and played Wembley Arena in front of sixteen thousand people which went down a storm. Roddy thought the gigs would dry up but everybody just carried on loving the music of the sixties and the nostalgia.

He was at home one evening when the phone range. His wife, Sandra, answered and said, "It's for you, it's your tour manager." Sandra never said the name of anyone who phoned whom she did not like and that was usually anyone connected with the music business.

"Hi Roddy, Bob here." Bob Johnson was the long-time manager of 'The Typhoons'. He would organise the tours, the rehearsals and the studio time when they were recording. He was also the 'go-to' guy for anything else, and I mean *anything*. "I know you have this weekend off but a promoter friend of mine has been let down in Belgium at an open air concert and he wants us to go over and headline it for him. You'll be working with all the boys - The Merseys, The Swinging Blue Jeans, The Searchers. It's completely sold out but he desperately needs a headline act to finish the concert off. Are you OK with that?"

Roddy was fine with that. He would rather be gigging this weekend than being reminded that the

133

grass needs cutting and there was a whole list of jobs that needed doing around the house.

When he told Sandra he had to work at the weekend, in the old days she would scream and shout, "what about the kids etc. etc.", but nowadays she just went quiet and they did not speak until he got back. Even then, it took a while. When they were speaking, she would say, "You're too old to be a rockstar, when are you going to pack it in?"

Roddy would just look at her because, truthfully, he would rather be gigging than sitting at home getting a load of old earache from the missus.

Everything went well for the gig. Punters used to say to him, "You get a grand for doing an hour's work. That's real kushty."

What they did not know was that the work started the morning he was due to travel. He had to pick his gig clothes from the dry cleaners, pack a suitcase with enough clothes, pants, and so on for the weekend and then drive to Heathrow Airport, a real ball ache, to meet up with the guys.

A one hour flight later, they landed in Brussels, were picked up in a minibus by the promoter and taken to their hotel, which just for once, was actually OK although for some strange reason, they had to cross the street to a local cafe for breakfast and for their evening meal. Roddy never ate before a gig anyway. It did not help with the nerves which he still got before he went on stage.

They sorted themselves out at the hotel and were then driven to the festival site to soundcheck and to run through a couple of numbers that were a bit ropey at last week's gig.

Roddy, a non-drinker, non-smoker and non-everything else turned round to the band and said, "Right, no drinking before the gig. The V.I.P. section will remain open for us after the finish of the concert to meet a few selected punters, sign autographs, do photos, the usual bullshit and there will be a free bar. You can get wrecked then."

One or two of the band gave him a look but they usually see sense in what he was saying. They went back to the band for a pre-gig sleep. He would introduce this into the band's itinerary after, he was told. Even from the early days, the Status Quo boys always had an hour's kip before their gigs. If it was good enough for Quo, it was good enough for The Typhoons.

The gig went brilliantly. There's nothing like a couple thousand sixties fans watching four of the top groups on tour. Everyone had perfected their art over the years and there were expert at raising the atmosphere to fever pitch. The Typhoons had to come back three times before the crowd would let them finally finish and all four guys came off drenched with sweat. Roddy was high on endorphins; the rest of the group were high on that as well, plus a few chemicals.

Roddy asked them once why they took drugs before a gig. Harry, the bass player explained, "You're guaranteed a great time even if you end up playing like crap and the gig's a bummer."

"But how do you know if the band has gone down well because we are a great band?"

"I don't know, and usually don't care, as long as I get paid and the royalties for record sales keep pouring in."

Roddy thought if he felt like that about performing, he would rather go back to teaching.

They were all at the bar of the V.I.P. room, talking to the promoter, signing a few autographs for the privileged few who had paid over the top for the privilege of meeting band members back stage.

Roddy turned round, took a sip of his drink, and then it happened. A vision was looking straight at him - an unbelievably gorgeous vision with long blonde hair, stunning green eyes, a body that promised everything on Earth.

At first, Roddy turned round because he thought she cannot be looking at him, surely?

"Hi, I just wanted tell you how much I enjoyed the show."

Roddy then did something he had never done in his life. He intended on bending over to shake hands and introduce himself but instead cupped her gorgeous face with his left hand to bring her closer and kissed her full on the lips. He had never known passion like it, the kiss was returned with equal feeling and when they finally parted and looked into each other's eyes, they both knew they had fallen in love without even a word being spoken.

This was it. This is what he hoped would happen to him all of his life. Love at first sight. Incredible.

He stuttered, "My name's Roddy," he blurted.

"I know your name, silly. I've been buying your records for years. I'm a big fan."

Roddy looked around him to see where they could sit, where they could be alone. Then he spotted them. One gold band and one diamond ring on her left hand. She was married!

"My name's 'Olga' and yes, I'm married. My husband's a policeman who moonlights helping with the security at all the concerts we have here in Brussels."

Roddy just stood there, stumped for words. "Can I buy you a drink?" was all he could think to say.

"I would rather go back to your hotel so we can talk." Music to Roddy's ears he quickly asked the roadie if he could take them to the hotel. Half an hour later, they were sitting in the cocktail lounge drinking coffee and staring into each other's eyes. There had not been much conversation in the back of the minibus as, basically, they could not keep their hands off of each other.

Roddy was still stunned. He had never felt like this before.

"I'm sorry, but it's getting late. I'll have to get back." She spoke with sadness in her eyes. They both knew all they wanted to do was to spend the night together. How could they make it possible?

Roddy had never, in all his married life, considered he was being unfaithful to his wife. They were just one night stands, a way of getting physical relief so he did not have to wake his wife up in the middle of the night after he came home from a gig. He had never known, until tonight, what it meant to be in love. His body still had not gotten over the shock of it.

Olga wrote on a piece of paper her mobile number and Facebook details so Roddy, over the next couple of weeks, was able to keep in touch.

"What's the matter with you lately?" asked Sandra. "You've been cutting the grass without being asked. You've even emptied the dishwasher!"

"Just trying to keep the peace, my love, just trying to keep the peace."

***

A few weeks later, Roddy received a call from Bob Johnson, the band's manager. "Hi Roddy, good news! The promoter in Belgium was so impressed with the band he's booked you into the Arts Centre. There'll be a few other acts but you'll be closing the first half."

Good, thought Roddy *I can nip off and spend some time with Olga.* Roddy asked Bob to change hotels for the Belgium gig.

"The hotel I've booked you into, Roddy, is a ten minute walk from the gig. The one you want is an hour away!"

"That's the one I want, Bob, just book it!"

Bob wondered what was going on. Roddy had never spoken to him like that before. In an effort to keep the peace, Bob did what Roddy asked but just could not see the sense in it.

The gig went well and Roddy rushed offstage and straight into a pre-booked taxi.

Upon arriving at the hotel, he went straight to the room where Olga was waiting.

Roddy had never experienced a night of passion like he shared with Olga that night. The first time they made love, they could not wait to take their clothes off and ended up on the floor. Afterwards, they giggled and went to bed. They talked and talked and the next time they made love, it was slow and gentle as though it was going to be the last time.

In the morning, Olga stayed in bed as Roddy got his things together ready for the band minibus to pick him up. They, once again, went over the arrangements they had planned the night before. There was no gig the following weekend so Roddy was going to tell Sandra they had been invited back to Belgium to do another show. Roddy was going to bring his suitcase and meet Olga in the cafe at the railway station as they were going to live together in the small apartment just outside Brussels that Olga used to commute to for work five days a week, as she normally went home every weekend. This would be the last time she would be going home as she would be telling her husband that she did not love him anymore and she was moving out. He could keep her share of the house they lived in. She would just make do with the flat. She would carry on with her work as a lawyer until Roddy could find a residency in a hotel or bar so he could carry on performing. The money did not matter. Their love was all that mattered. Their love was all-consuming to the extent that perhaps they had not thought everything through thoroughly.

Everything went ahead as planned. Roddy was sitting in the railway cafe waiting for Olga, trying to compose a letter to Sandra as did not have the guts to tell her out about Olga to her face.

Roddy looked up as the cafe door opened expecting it to be Olga as she was late. Instead, it was a policeman who walked straight over to Roddy's table, sat down, took out his Ruger semi-automatic 9mm pistol, and placed it on the table in front of him.

"Just shut up and listen. Don't utter a sound or I'll shoot you. Nod if you understand."

Roddy nodded like a toy dog. He had never been threatened with a gun before and, to be honest, he was scared to death.

"Do you honestly think you're the first pop star Olga's lusted after? You're the third that I know of. Did she tell you we have eleven year-old twin girls? No, I bet she didn't. Who the hell do you think you are, a couple of teenagers? Do you think I'm going to give her half the house, half the flat? They're both in my name. Do you think I'm stupid?

Do you think I can go to work when they hear my wife's run off with an ageing popstar? I'm up for promotion. What do you think a messy divorce is going to do to my chances?"

Roddy went to speak, but the policeman just held his hand up. "Don't even think about saying anything. Apart from your sordid little encounter screwing up my life and the life of our daughters, how about your shitty life? Does your wife know you're leaving her? I bet she doesn't. I can tell weak-minded cowards, with no back bone, a mile off. After I've contacted my friends at Interpol, do you think your band will be safe the next time you gig across the water? I'll have every gig raided for drugs. It'll get so bad, no promoter will dare book you again. English promoters as well will be wary. It'll affect your fan base when the tabloids print everything I'm going to send them. Nod your head if you're getting all of this."

Roddy nodded his head and was in shock at what he was hearing.

"I've told Olga all of this and I've left her crying her heart out as she has done several times before. I've told her and I'm telling you now, Olga and I are staying married until my girls go off to university then she can do what the hell she likes. Do you think she'll wait that long for you? No chance. She'll need someday younger by then. What age will you be? 80 years old? There won't be a lot of passion left then, will there? So, Mr. Popstar, you go straight back to your wife, to your children, to your beloved grandchildren and, I'm warning you, don't even think of coming back to Belgium ever again."

With that, he stood up, lifted his pistol from the table, momentarily pointed it straight at Roddy's head just to make his final point and walked out of the cafe.

Roddy then did two things.

He went straight home to his family.

He left the band.

I don't think any of them lived happily ever after.

Cold Revenge

In the old days, back in the 1960's, people used to go to pubs. No Sky TV, no mobile phones, no cheap slabs of beer so you can stay in and watch Premier League football. In fact, there was no Premier League Football. Pubs were great back then. With nothing to do in the house after eating dinner, if you wanted to meet up with your mates, you went down to the pub. They would all be there. No Facebook or Whats App to contact them. They would just be there. Drink, by golly, they would drink. Work hard but play harder was the rule. Get drunk, then go home to sleep it off before the next day at work.

At the centre of all this culture was the pub landlord. He was the one who said who could come in, who was barred, and who, if anyone, had too much to drink. Customers would drink so much that the beer was delivered in tanks, not barrels. Tankers, similar to the petrol tankers of today, would turn up at the cellar doors, hoses would be undone and taken down to the cellar and attached to the empty tanks, which had been meticulously cleaned, to give the pub landlord yet another week's supply of booze.

Whisky was the 'top shelf' drink of choice. No alcopops, no cocktails, and certainly no wine. Pubs did not serve wine in those days. Gin and tonics? I don't think so. If you wanted a carry out at the end of the night, it was a large seven pint container called a 'Party 7'. Seven more pints of beer to be getting on with when you got home. If you wanted to 'get in' with the wife, you would take home a Babycham for her with a packet of plain crisps. No flavoured crisps in those days.

Your average pub landlord, in those days, would be six-foot tall, six-feet round and enough sovereigns on his fingers to start a rush on the price of gold.

Philip Marsh, 32 years old, 'Pip' to his mates, was one such landlord. Married to Anne, with no kids, they had been running The Nags Head for three years, it has to be said very successfully as was displayed proudly by the plaque on the wall behind the bar: The Nags Head, Brinkley, Pub Of The Year. Because they lived in the pub rent free and did not have to pay the normal household bills, Pip was able to buy a brand new Mk9 Jaguar which seemed to be the usual pub landlord's car of choice.

Like most couples running pubs back in the day, they came from a showbiz background. Anne had been a 'Tiller Girl', her long legs used to dance in many Variety shows and even graced the stage of the London Palladium. Pip had been the singer in a rock 'n roll band and still loved to belt out his favourite songs on 'Free 'n Easy' nights. No karaoke in those days, just Fred on the accordion who could play anything you asked for as long as there was a whisky for him in your hand.

By the time Pip and Anne rang the bell behind the bar and called "last orders, please," served their last customers, helped the staff clean up, wash the glasses, and they had counted the tills, it was well-past midnight. They always treated the barmaids who worked for them to a staff drink and then it was Pip's job to run the staff home, not getting back until about 12.30pm. There was a rumour that whichever barmaid got dropped off last would spend some rather exciting time in the back seat of Pip's Jag.

Now do not forget there was no such thing as breathalysers back in the day, so Pip would not give a second thought to how much he had had to drink. In fact, if truth be told, Pip thought he drove his big Mk9 Jaguar better when he had a couple of beers.

Pip had to get up early to let the cleaners in at 6am. He would reconcile the tills, put the takings in the safe, and by the time Anne came downstairs, he was ready for his morning cup of coffee. Unknown to Anne, Pip always put what he called a 'livener' into his coffee in the shape of a large brandy.

As this particular day was a Tuesday, Pip would make his weekly trip to the Cash 'n Carry to buy stock for the pub, crisps etc. To this day, Pip cannot really remember what happened. He was waiting at the edge of the pub car park for a space in the flow of traffic to appear when, somehow, his foot slipped on the throttle pedal and the car shot forward.

**

Tom McClelland, the local Headmaster of Brinkley Junior School, was a true gent in every sense of the word. Immaculate with suit, collar and tie, he always made a point of wearing his university robes when he addressed early morning assembly. Not quite six-foot tall his gaunt, thin face gave him rather a sombre look but when he praised his pupils, his face would break into a lovely warm smile.

Although his school only taught children up to age seven and juniors up to eleven, he still thought it was important to give the right impression to the youngsters who all looked up at him in awe. If 'Sir' was walking the corridors of school during break, there was no running, shouting, or misbehaving. The man had that effect on the children and staff, and as a result, the school had an excellent reputation. Married late in life, he was now 56 years old and as Heather, his wife, who was the local GP, was 40 years old when he met her, it came as a massive, but really pleasant surprise when she announced she was pregnant only nine months after they were married.

Daniel, their son, was eight and had been in the junior school for a year now and doing well. He struggled with Maths in particular but, by working hard, he managed to achieve good grades in all of his subjects and what really mattered to Daniel was he excelled at football and was tipped to be the school's captain in the following year.

That fateful morning, it was a lovely Spring day. Still a bit chilly from what had been an unusually harsh winter, the sky was a beautiful blue with not a cloud in the sky giving you a clue which way the wind was blowing. Tom was driving Heather's MINI Clubman that morning as his Rover 2000 was in getting serviced. There was no seat belts in the new 1966 vehicle as only new cars were being fitted with belts in the early seventies. It became compulsory later on; and later still for rear belts to be fitted.

With Heather in the passenger seat and Daniel rummaging around in his school satchel to make sure he remembered his reading book and pencil box, Tom was driving carefully along the High Street at the allowed speed of 30mph. He often told Daniel that when he learned to drive, whatever it said on the road sign should read the same as what is shown on the car's speedometer as most bad accidents are caused by excessive speed. Daniel always listened attentively to his father when he talked about driving as it was his dream, as with all the other boys in his class, that one day he would drive his own car. That said, Tom was not pleased when his son put a picture up in his bedroom of his favourite car, the Jaguar E-Type, which was capable of 150 mph.

Tom slowed even further as he passed the row of shops on the left-hand side of the High Street, conscious of early morning shoppers and children walking to school. He only managed to see, out of his right-hand peripheral vision, the large saloon car that was the Jaguar Mk9 accelerating towards him.

Pip's reactions were not quick enough to avoid the collision, mainly due to last night's booze and this morning's double brandy. Thus, the Jaguar was still accelerating when it struck the driver's door. Although the Mini was only going 30mph, combined with the speed of the Jaguar, the impact speed must have been nearer to 50mph. The body shell of the Mini was no match for the bulk of the Jaguar and the Mk9 crushed the Mini as though it was made of cardboard.

The first thing that happened in the first millisecond of the accident was Tom's right ankle was snapped in two. Then the bonnet of the Jaguar, on its way to the far side of the small vehicle, crushed the right-hand side of Tom's ribcage. The broken ribs tore into Tom's heart and split open his aorta causing the twelve pints of blood to bleed out in a matter of minutes. Death for Tom was instantaneous. His body was thrown sideways and, unfortunately, collided with Heather's, which was rebounding off her doorway. Both of their heads collided causing instantaneous severe fractures to the side of Heather's skull. Daniel was lucky. With no seat belt to restrain him, he was thrown forward into the well behind the passenger's seat. He was still conscious but severely shaken.

Pip had suffered no injuries whatsoever as his brand new Jaguar had absorbed the majority of the impact. He sat in shock looking at the wreckage he had caused. Already people were trying the doors of the Mini to release the badly injured passengers.

"I'll go and phone for an ambulance," Pip shouted as he ran back into the pub breathlessly telling Anne what had happened and to get him a brandy quick as he was in shock. Anne phoned the ambulance service who, in turn, in the case of bad road accidents, contacted the police to attend.

The ambulance took all three of the Mini's occupants to Salford A&E. It was in response to the policeman's first question, "Had he been drinking?" that Pip decided he had to lie to get himself out of what could be a very bad situation.

"No," said Pip.

"Your breathe smells of alcohol sir," stated the policeman.

It was Anne who answered, "He was in such a state when he came in to phone the ambulance that I gave him a double brandy to help calm him down."

Tom was pronounced dead on arrival at the hospital. Heather managed to hang on for two more days before she succumbed to her injuries. As there was no response whatsoever in Heather's brain, the decision was made to switch off the machine which kept her alive.

Daniel was still in the children's ward as the doctors wanted to be sure there were no internal injuries and also give social services enough time to find someone to look after the lad now that both his parents had gone.

***

All these memories came flooding back to Daniel as he stood by his Jaguar E-Type that he had just parked in the car park of The Nags Head pub. It was exactly 20 years since the day of the accident and he thought he would visit the place where he had lost his mum and dad if only to stop the nightmares he was still having in his late-twenties.

His foster parents had been brilliant. They had an elder son, Jon, who soon became Daniel's beloved brother. In fact, when Jon decided to leave school to join the R.A.F., Daniel decided that would be the career for him as well.

Daniel excelled in the R.A.F. His prowess on the playing fields was a good skill to transfer to flying Tornado jets at ground level travelling at Mach 1.

One day, he was called into his squadron leader's office.

"Daniel, I've brought you in today to offer you a choice of promotions. The first I can offer you is a position with the Red Arrows or I can offer you six months training at Holloman Air Force Base in New Mexico where you will train to fly our latest drones. After six months, you will be transferred back to R.A.F. Waddington to finish your training on the weapon side of flying the drones and you will be put on active service."

"Active service, sir, taking out targets and such?"

"Exactly, young man. These drones can pinpoint enemies who are just leaving their houses or travelling in their cars. The drones, when flown properly, are extremely accurate and effective."

"All sounds a bit cold-blooded, sir."

"You're right, we need you to be as cold-blooded as you can be. Nothing should be allowed to interfere with your ability to take out recognised targets."

"What about civilian casualties if one day I'm not as accurate as I should be?"

"Civilian casualties are exactly that, casualties of war. Sometimes it just cannot be helped. A drone attack is the best way to take out insurgents whilst minimising the risk of any other kind of casualties. The civilian population should be protected as much as is humanly possible. Just remember one dead civilian means a dozen new committed terrorists."

***

Daniel's first kill was five males travelling in a black limousine. When the dust settled after the explosion, there was nothing left, just a pile of debris where there was once a car with five occupants.

His second kill, he was told, was a man and wife. The male was a high-ranking member of ISIS. His wife was also involved. She was seen in one of their beheading videos helping to hold the prisoner down whilst he was being executed. Daniel used these videos as motivation for being as cold-blooded and accurate as he could be and he soon became the assassin of choice with his commanding officers. Daniel got over the sickening feeling that he would spend all day helping to win the war against terrorism and in the evening enjoy a fine meal, served with a good bottle of wine, in the officers' mess.

It must have been the same for the Spitfire pilots in the Second World War - one minute murdering a fellow human being, next minute enjoying a pint down the pub with your mates. Daniel had learned over time how to separate the two. He was at war and he clung onto the feeling he was doing his duty for Queen and country.

So it was a very different man who entered The Nags Head pub that day, very different from the eight year old boy mown down on his way to school.

"Pint of Bitter please," Daniel asked for his drink as he looked around the typical British boozer. *Needs a bloody good clean for a start,* thought Daniel.

"You're a stranger, aren't ya? Haven't seen you in here before," enquired the barmaid. She was quite an attractive woman…. well she might have been when she was younger. Smoking had added a few lines on her face and Daniel assumed the blonde hair now came out of a bottle.

"Not exactly a stranger. I used to live here in Brinkley."

'Whereabouts?" asked the barmaid.

"Just down the road a couple of miles in Rose Cottage. I was the school headmaster's son."

"You're not the young boy who lost both parents in the car accident outside the pub are you?"

"The very same," replied Daniel taking a sup of his lukewarm beer.

"I'm the landlady here now but back then I was one of the part-time barmaids."

"So you must have known the landlord and landlady back then?"

"Oh yes, very well. Pip and Anne moved to another pub, as Pip had too many bad memories for him to carry on working here."

"Do you remember what happened that day?"

"I know exactly what happened. Pip had a large brandy every morning, hair of the dog sort of thing, to try and curb the massive hangovers he used to get."

Daniel could not believe what he just heard. All his life, he believed it was an awful accident and no one was at fault, as the police did not charge anyone. Perhaps the police never checked on the landlord's drinking habits. They had no proof he had been drinking earlier that day and the previous night. The breathalyser was not introduced until the following year.

From what the landlady was saying, the man had caused the death of his parents whilst driving heavily under the influence of alcohol. But the man had made a statement. He said the policeman could smell alcohol on his breathe. His wife claimed she had given him a large brandy as he was in shock after seeing what damage the accident had done to the car and the occupants. He had avoided justice and whilst carrying on working as a pub landlord.

"Do you know where they are now?"

"They're running City Limits, a big music pub near Star City in Birmingham. It's a busy boozer."

Daniel thanked her for her help. He was determined to find the man who killed his parents. The first thing he did was to ring his Commanding Officer and ask for some personal leave time.

"Should only be a couple of weeks, sir. I have a very important family matter to sort out."

"No problem, you've got a few weeks leave due to you anyway. Take your time, Daniel, you've been working really hard lately. Take all the time you need."

"Thank you, sir." Daniel pressed the 'off' button on his mobile phone. His smile was more like a grimace when he recounted his boss comparing 'working hard' to 'murdering strangers'.

Daniel visited City Limits a couple of times over the next week, once during the day and then once at night when the pub was hosting an 'open mic' night. He had noticed the landlord, a huge man with a large belt to keep his stomach from hanging down, a heart attack waiting to happen. He was always the wrong side of bar, pint in hand, chatting to the customers.

Because of its proximity to the nightlife centre at the outskirts of Birmingham, the pub was busy at night, and not so busy during the day. There was a typical pub food operation but when Daniel's curry was delivered on the plate with the rice still in the bag unopened, Daniel decided not to eat there again.

In his spare time, Daniel loved to play his beloved white Fender Stratocaster and he had often, alongside a couple of other musicians, played some gigs in the officers' mess. They went down really well due to Daniel's vocals, his superb guitar rifts, and the fact that he played all the Rock classics. The Who, The Stones, Free - you name it, he could play it. So he decided the best way to 'introduce himself' to the pub was to turn up on an open mic night and just get up and play. He would then ask the landlord if there was free beer for the musicians and see where it went from there.

Needless to say, Daniel's guitar playing went down a storm. The resident drummer knew all of Daniel's songs and the bass player was over the moon to show off playing John Entwistle's bass solo in the cover of The Who's 'My Generation'.

Pip, the landlord of City Limits and the ex-landlord of The Nags Head, was mightily impressed by Daniel's musicianship. He gladly poured Daniel a free pint when Daniel had approached him.

"What are you doing this Saturday? A band has let me down. Do you fancy doing the gig?"

"I've just come up from London to start my Masters degree in Music at Birmingham University. I haven't even sorted out my accommodation yet."

"You look a bit old to be a student."

"I've tried for years to 'make it' in the music business down in London. I've given up all hope now and when I get my degree, I'll just be teaching music instead of playing it."

"What a waste," replied Pip. "Can you do the gig?"

"Sure," replied Daniel, "but I haven't got anywhere to stay yet. I'm staying at a local Premier Inn but it's too expensive. I don't suppose you have any cheap rooms?"

"You're in luck. I fell out with my head barman last week. He was giving the stock away to his mates instead of taking their money. You can have his room. It's not much, single bed, one set of drawers."

"I've worked in pubs to put myself through Uni a few years back when I was studying for my degree so I can do a few shifts, if it helps you out? I haven't got any mates in the area so I won't be giving your stock away."

Pip laughed at this and said, "You're on, let me show you the room."

Pip was right when he said the room was not much. The only plus side was that it was next door to the pub's boiler room so Daniel was always dry and nice and warm.

The question was when was the right time to ask Pip about the accident. Daniel decided if there was an element of contrition, he would just report him to the police and see that justice was done. If there wasn't, Daniel decided he was going to kill him. All he had to do was to find a way to do so. Because of his job, Daniel had no problem killing people on a regular basis as long as the powers to be convinced him the world would be a better place without men prepared to behead another human being proudly showing off in front of a TV camera.

The first few days went by and Daniel had never been so busy. He volunteered to take over the Head Barman's duties which included changing barrels in the cellar, stocking the shelves with the bottled beer, Coca Cola and fruit juices, cleaning out the glass washer at the end of every shift, washing down the cellar and cleaning the beer lines, etc. Daniel was a quick learner and, funnily enough, he was getting on well with Pip especially when, on Saturday night in the middle of Daniel's set, Pip jumped on stage to sing The Troggs' classic 'Wild Thing' which not only brought the house down, but brought Pip's trousers down to below his knees accompanied by hoots of laughter from the audience. Pip was too pissed to notice. He just loved singing.

It was halfway through the second week, in the middle of a reasonably quiet Tuesday night, that Daniel asked Pip how he and Anne got into the pub game. Anne had not been around when Daniel started at the pub. She was 'up north' caring for her ailing mother. "No problem there, bud. While the cat's away, the mice will play," Pip said whilst looking at a really nice rear view of one of the new barmaids.

"Well, we always fancied the pub trade so when we were offered a start at a small village pub, The Nags Head in Brinkley, it proved to be a good opportunity to learn all the skills required running what I've always considered to be a small business. Bookwork, stock control, cash control, selecting, and training, hiring the right staff and, on top of this, always keeping your beer spot on. A fresh pint in a clean glass goes a long way in turning a visitor into a regular."

Daniel could see why Pip was successful in doing what he was doing. He certainly knew his stuff. Daniel decided not to press him that night as Pip was sober for a change and Daniel had a feeling that he had to get him drunk for him to find out the truth about what happened on that fateful day back in 1966.

***

City Limits was originally an 18th century coaching inn and had been used as an overnight stop with travellers coming down from the north of England breaking up their journey down to London. Like all pubs built originally for this purpose, they all had large areas for stagecoaches to pull in to rest the horses for the night so they also had outer buildings for stabling. The main drink was beer so the pubs had big cellars to accommodate large deliveries of barrels. City Limits was an ideal pub to expand and had sufficient car parking spaces in what was still a large car parking area. The stable block now housed the live entertainment venue whereas the bar and restaurant was located in what was the original pub. The cellar was the same floor size as the bar and restaurant.

One of the last jobs after a busy night was to go down to the cellar, stack the empty barrels to one side and roll fresh barrels next to the dispensing units for when the next barrel would run out. Changing barrels was a messy business. They were pressurised to 22 P.S.I. to enable the staff to draw the beer up to the beer taps and to do this, they were connected to gas cylinders. The cylinders were about three feet high, ten inches round and, when full of compressed air, they were quite heavy to lift. Swopping an empty barrel onto a full one always meant that a few pints of beer ended up on the floor. So the final job of the night was to wash the cellar floor down so it was clean and tidy for next day's trading. The barrels themselves were delivered by the breweries' draymen who would manhandle them to the cellar doors, located in the car park, and gently lower them by rope down the steep steps onto the cellar floor.

The cellar steps were edged with steel to protect the concrete steps from being damaged by the weight of a thirty-six gallon barrel of beer. The cellar doors were always padlocked to prevent entry into the pub from the outside car park.

It was going to be Daniel's last night working at the pub. His leave was up and he had to report back to R.A.F. Wadington on Monday. It was the usual busy Saturday night and Daniel had been working behind the bar from the start of shift at 6pm until calling last orders at midnight.

Pip had done his usual. He drank with the customers and only had a break when he got onstage with the band and gave an enthusiastic version of Eddie Cochran's 'Summertime Blues'. Daniel thought this had to be the night when, finally, Pip would get his comeuppance for killing Daniel's parents.

Daniel offered to run the staff home so Pip could take advantage of having a 'lock in' where he invited favoured customers to stay for a late, late drink. This went on until two in the morning. Daniel pretended to drink the brandies that Pip kept buying and, one by one, the customers drifted away.

When it was just Pip and Daniel left, Daniel chose his moment. "Tell me again, Pip, how you got started in the pub trade as I'm thinking of getting a pub of my own one day."

"Do you think you'll be good enough, young Daniel? You have to be all things to all men. One minute you're entertaining the customers, next thing you're checking the tills to make sure you haven't been robbed and then, in the morning, you have to

160

be a bloody accountant to make sure the books balance. One set of books for you and another set for the brewery. How do think I'm able to afford the Jag and a villa in Spain? On the measly salary the brewery pay me, no chance." Pip tapped the side of his nose to emphasise that it was alright for him to swindle the brewery. It's not all show business, you know."

"You started in a smaller pub, didn't you? The Nags Head at Brinkley, I think you said. Did that make you much money?"

"We were doing alright until that bloody accident."

"What accident was that?" asked Daniel, trying to sound as naive as possible.

"It was when I was going to Cash 'n Carry. I had to remember this, remember that. I had a real skinful the night before so I had a bit of the 'hair of the dog' the next morning, a cup of coffee mixed with a large brandy. God knows what happened but I manage to crash my Mk 9 Jag into the local headmaster's Mini. You know those Mini's, they haven't got a proper steel chassis like the Jag, just a square sub frame to stick four wheels on. Bloody useless in a collision. My car went through them like a knife through butter. Killed him and his missus more or less instantaneously. They had an eight year old lad who survived."

"Were you convicted for dangerous driving?" Daniel asked. He thought he had said too much as

Pip's eyes narrowed and he moved his chair a bit closer to where Daniel was sitting.

"You think I'm bloody stupid? I just told the policeman I hadn't been drinking and only had a brandy after the accident because I was in shock."

"Weren't you worried about the occupants of the car?"

"Couldn't do much for them. There was blood everywhere. I've never seen so much carnage. What I was most worried about was getting caught by the police."

Daniel was finding it difficult to control his anger. "You said you were doing alright until that accident. What happened afterwards?"

"You see, I was knocking off one of the barmaids at the time, a real cracker she was. Well, she wanted me to leave Anne and run a pub with her. I told her, "That ain't never going to happen," so she stared blabbing about how much I'd had to drink the night before and drinking again in the morning. It got so bad that many of the customers stopped coming in and trade was lousy. So I just decided to hop it before the rumours reached the ears of the local constabulary."

"So you literally got away with murder?"

"I suppose you could say that," Pip laughed when he said it.

Daniel's demeanour rapidly changed. If Pip had any idea what Daniel really did for a living, he may have recognised the danger signs. The coldness in the stare, the way his tongue stuck out slightly when he was concentrating.

"Shit!" exclaimed Daniel. "I haven't finished doing the cellar."

"Just do it in the morning, it'll be alright."

"Sunday mornings the only shift I have off. Come on, if you give me a hand, we'll have it done in no time at all."

"Alright then, you'll have to help me get up, though." He laughed again as he staggered slightly getting to his feet.

Down in the cellar, Daniel grabbed the floor brush and started to swill and sweep the floor with clean water. "It's only that barrel of lager that needs changing for the morning, I've done the rest."

Pip bent down to unscrew the gas fitting on the barrel. As he did so, Daniel lifted one of the nearby gas cylinders. With perfect timing as Pip stood up, Daniel crashed the full gas bottle on the back of Pip's skull. It was as easy as breaking an egg with a similar sound. Pip collapsed to the floor. Daniel climbed the concrete steps up to the outer cellar doors and unlocked the padlock. He pushed one, then the other, open. There was no one in the car park.

Daniel had a good look around to see if there was anyone about and then went back down the cellar steps and attached the draymen's rope to the body of Pip and dragged him over to the bottom of the steps. He went to the top and with several might heaves, he managed to get the body out and onto to ground of the car park. He then threw the rope back down the steps into the cellar.

Pip was a big man. A typical pub landlord of the old school. Long hours in the gym though paid off for Daniel as he managed to get Pip to his feet, face him over the opening of the cellar and with one last effort, threw him down the stairs. It was like slow motion as, first of all, Pip's head hit one of the steel edgings and split open. The dead weight of Pip's body was doing its job. When he fell onto his body, his arm was tucked awkwardly under his torso and Daniel enjoyed the sound of breaking bones as Pip's right arm snapped in two. Pip crashed onto the cellar floor. A pool of blood was forming around his head. His injuries, including the blow to the back of his head that had originally killed him, were conducive to the type of injuries a body would incur falling heavily downstairs whilst drunk onto steel-rimmed concrete stairs.

Daniel was more than satisfied. Satisfaction seemed to be the only feeling he had after he killed insurgents with his drone and now he felt exactly the same. Those terrorists deserved to die and so did Pip.

Daniel looked to the sky as he walked away from the pub for good. "Sorry Dad, I know you wouldn't approve. I'm not like you, Dad. I had to have my cold revenge."

The Court Case

Roger and Susan Hastings are in bed together. The bedroom is clearly decorated by a woman with a sense of mature style. They have been married for forty-one years, with two children, Thomas and Harriet. Roger is retired and Susan is still working. Both are in their mid-sixties. Susan is prim and slim, immaculate, but for various oily skin creams she applies every night before bed. She is an attractive woman, and only really shows her age in her expression of near permanent annoyance. She is reading a novel, a bodice ripper of some sort. Roger is a man of small frame with a kind face that is offset slightly by a look of resignation in his eyes.

Roger turns to look at his wife. Ignoring the oily skin, he makes an advance on his wife obviously seeking affection.

"Stop it." Susan doesn't even look up from her book. Roger continues to try his luck.

"Stop it. I'm trying to read for God's sake."

She shuffles away from him, her permanent air of annoyance clearly shown by a sideways glance that if held for more than a minute or two, would turn Roger, or anyone within ten metres, into a pillar of salt.

Roger turned over, obviously sulking, feeling sorry for himself. He felt cheated, and angry, at the constant bedroom rejection. He could not remember the last time they had made love. He thought back to when they had first met. Susan had insisted that they would have to wait until they got married before they went 'the whole way' and Roger could clearly remember walking up the aisle on their wedding day thinking *"Yahoo! Tonight's the night."*

He made one last attempt only to be met with rejection and the words, "Stop it, I'm trying to read."

"You're trying to read? Not a headache, then? You're not tired or washing your hair?"

"Stop being unreasonable, Roger. I've nearly finished this chapter. Maybe tomorrow night."

"When did it come to this? When did we start scheduling our sex life? Are you sure tomorrow's fine? Are you sure you can squeeze me in?"

Susan is clearly not paying attention.

"Of course, Darling. Now go to sleep. Don't forget you've got the garden to do tomorrow."

Roger retreats, obviously unhappy with his lot.

The following morning, Roger is taking a break from his gardening duties. He is sitting on the doorstep of the back door, coffee in one hand, stroking the family dog, a Cockapoo called Minxie, with the other. He gazes at the quality of the lawn he has just mowed. It provided a superb centerpiece to their garden and Roger is convinced that Andy Murray could play his next Wimbledon final on its immaculate surface.

Roger starts talking to the dog which looks up at him hoping for a treat as well as his tummy getting rubbed.

"Well Minxie, when did a Mills & Boon novel take my place as the romantic interest? Did it happen overnight? Forty-one years of marriage and you forget who you really are. Amidst the careers and the mortgages, the kids and the college fees, you stop being Sue and Rog. Good ol' Sue and Rog who might go dancing just for the hell of it, who might have a drink or three with their friends, who once made love outside a police station. No, Sue and Rog died a long time ago, swamped under by nest-eggs and board meetings, dinner parties, deadlines and designer dogs. We are Mr. and Mrs. Hastings. Proud parents and hard workers. A poster couple for the upper middle class. We have furniture from Harrods. We have bathroom fittings from Italy. We have stupid post-modern art works from Ikea. We have about as much sex as a nun on Christmas Day. What do you do when romantic novels take your place?"

Roger looked down as he heard a strange sound. It was the dog snoring contentedly on his lap. Blooming heck! He could not even get the dog to understand his frustrations.

Roger returns his empty coffee cup to the kitchen which is fitted with an army of expensive appliances, very rarely used, and where Susan is finishing getting ready for work. She is clearly a professional, wearing a power-suit that is obviously very expensive.

As she fusses around her morning coffee, she kicks Minxie, the irksome Cockapoo, away from under her feet. Susan then goes into the downstairs bathroom to put some finishing touches to her hair and make-up.

Roger picks up Minxie and starts, once again, speaking to the dog. "Look at her, Minxie. She's a professional with a capital 'P'. From the Gucci power-suit to the gold shoes imported from Spain, the image says it all. Regional Director for Spring Cosmetics, Chairperson of the local Women's Institute, long-term heavyweight on the Village Parish Council. Watching her get ready for work tires me out for the rest of the day."

"Don't forget to take Minxie for her morning walk, Roger."

"Yes dear," replied Roger.

"You forget to do so yesterday and she ended up peeing all over our new Persian rug."

"I know dear." Roger started to nod his head like the dog on the car insurance adverts.

"Will you be playing golf with Thomas today?"

"Ah! Yes." Roger started to imitate Churchill's voice from the car adverts knowing full well Susan would not even notice.

"Make sure and remind him about the family dinner on Sunday, won't you?"

"Ah! Yes." More nodding dog.

"I'm off then. We need more milk and coffee, not the cheap stuff either! The lady at the shop knows what I like. Again, don't forget to take the dog out for its walk."

Susan leaves the house in a whirlwind of scheduled professionalism. Roger picks up Minxie and as he attaches her lead to her collar, he has one last moan about his unsatisfactory life.

"You put your life on hold for the sake of the house, the children, your job, and it never occurs to you to ask yourself what ever happened to Sue and Rog? What happened to the woman who once loved me with a passion that has since long faded away?" Minxie was too excited about the forthcoming walk to listen and she had to bark a couple of times to get Roger out of his trance.

***

At the golf course later on in the day, Roger is not playing very well as he scuffs yet another drive off the tee.

"Bad luck, Dad, what's up with you today?"

Tom, Roger's son, is thirty-six years old, six-foot tall and handsome in a smug sort of way, whereas Roger wears a pair of old plus four trousers and an old-fashioned golf jumper. Tom looks as though he has bought all the latest fashion gear from the Pro Shop and is wearing it all at once.

"Luck hasn't got anything to do with how I play golf. It takes years of practice to get this bad."

"You should chill out a bit more, Dad. Try and relax. It'll help improve your swing. You look terrible by the way."

"Thanks very much, son, that makes me feel a lot better. I didn't get much sleep last night as it happens. I've been feeling a bit down lately to tell you the truth."

Tom takes his shot. A perfect drive off the tee. Two hundred yards plus down the middle of the fairway. He pumps his fist into the air in an irritatingly smug manner. They both begin to walk up the fairway towards their balls.

"Sorry Dad, what were you saying?"

"Nothing Tom, don't worry about it. How's life in the Big City treating you?"

"Same old, same old, Dad, you know. Working a lot. Working hard."

Whilst he was saying this, Tom's mind brought up an image of himself 'working hard', mainly him and his mates downing 'Shooters' in a noisy and energetic London nightclub.

"Well, I should imagine things can be quite tough in the financial advisor game. Any girlfriends at the moment?"

"Nah! Not really. Well, there is one."

"Oh, really! What's her name?"

Tom has another flashback. He is sitting in a seedy strip club, most of his features obscured by the buttocks of a lap dancer. He holds a drink in one hand, a fifty in the other, and has a huge smile on his face.

"Her name's Tiara, I think, we've only recently just met."

Swiftly changing the subject, Tom asks Roger, "So haven't you got something to tell me?"

Roger looked puzzled.

"Oh! Come on Dad, you know the routine - we play golf, I beat you, you tell me not to forget about Sunday dinner at yours and Mum's every week. So it has been written, and so it shall be."

"Actually, Tom, I don't think there will be any Sunday dinner this week."

Tom is puzzled. He looks up from his next shot.

"Dad, how long have we known each other?"

"Well, all your life, obviously," replied Roger.

"Exactly - and in all that time, thirty-six years, can you name me one Sunday that hasn't been dictated by the brutal hegemony of Mum cooking Sunday dinner?"

'Well….' Roger goes to speak but hesitates.

"Come on Dad, six o'clock as usual, yeah?"

Roger spoke at last. "There really won't be any Sunday dinner."

"There are only a few things that could stop Mum's Sunday dinners, Dad, either a direct meteorite strike or…."

"Divorce?" replied Roger.

Tom was halfway through his swing when he heard the word 'divorce'. The club left his hands ending up in a nearby lake and, for the first time in his adult life, Tom was left speechless.

"I'm divorcing your mother. I am also suing her for 'False Promise'."

***

Later in the afternoon when Susan returned home from work, she notices a handwritten note has been left on the fridge door. She, at first, scans it rather hurriedly and then, frowning, takes the note from the fridge for a closer look.

Susan, finally comprehending the contents of the note, has just the right amount of time to look outraged and horrified after reading the word 'divorce' before she passes out onto the kitchen floor, face first, into Minxie's bowl of expensive dog food.

***

Later that day in a dark murky sex shop, with a thrash metal rock track playing in the background and a variety of 'interesting' toys adjourning the walls, Harry, the proprietor, is impatiently serving a last minute customer. Harriet Hastings, a good-looking woman of thirty-three years with a punky haircut and a raunchy sense of dress far too young for her, is getting fed up showing a long list of 'products' to a rather timid, middle-aged lady. The lady is obviously intimidated by the shop's surroundings and politely asks, "Haven't you got anything a bit smaller?"

Harry rolls her eyes and replaces the monstrous dildo she has just displayed back on the shelf. She selects another slightly smaller one.

"How about this? The 'Housewives Helper'."

Harry whacks the rubber dildo on the counter. The woman jumps slightly at the smacking sound.

"A sturdy classic favoured by those of a more traditional disposition. It's not the most innovative of designs but it gets the job done."

The lady customer feeling more embarrassed by the minute looks around the shop, then leans over the counter, and asks, "Erm.... have you got anything a little less phallic?"

Harry rolls her eyes again and replaces the dildo back on the shelf.

"Look, what you see is what we've got. A selection of dildos, vibrators, butt plugs, body lubricants in both edible and scented varieties, we have soft porn, bucket loads of hard porn, we have love beads, love eggs...."

"They sound about right."

"What, all of them?!" asked Harriet incredulously.

"No! God, no! The last one, the love eggs."

"An excellent choice," said Harry selecting the requested item from the shelf.

"They're round, smooth and easy to use! Just pop them into your piece, take a walk around Sainsbury's and you'll be sloshing your socks in no time."

"But are they any good?" asks the lady customer.

Harry looks thoughtful and then shifts her hips slightly. "They're not bad actually."

The woman looks disgusted and marches out of the store. Later, as Harry is locking up, the telephone rings and she shouts for her shop assistant, Sharon, to answer it.

Sharon picks up the phone and says, "Hello, this is 'Plug You In Play Pen, your 'One Stop Shop for a Substitute Cock', how can I help you?"

"Hey Sharon, it's Tom. Is Harry there? I need to speak to her urgently."

"It's not that Sunday dinner thing again, is it?"

"No Sharon, it isn't, mainly because it's Saturday. Just tell her it's vital she gets to Mum's house as soon as possible, OK?!"

Sharon then hangs up the phone and calls to Harry. "Harry, that's your brother, he says it's urgent that you get to your Mum's house as soon as possible."

"Christ, it's not Sunday already, is it?" Harry scrambles around looking for her car keys and departs in a hurry.

On arriving at her parent's home, Harry lets herself in the front door, careful to make sure her punky hair is covered by a floppy hat and her raunchy clothes hidden by a long shapeless coat.

She walks into the kitchen calling for her Mum. She's confused as the kitchen is in a bit of a mess, certainly not in its usual showroom condition, with dog food splattered everywhere.

She walks upstairs and, after some searching, finds her mum sitting on her bed in a dressing gown, tears streaming down her un-made face.

Her mum turns, sees that it's Harry, stands up to hug her and in-between tears, cries, "Oh Harriet, my little Harriet."

Harry is stunned and unsure how to react. Her mum hadn't hugged her since the infants school.

"What am I going to do? What am I going to do?"

"Look, chill out, Mum, what's wrong? Did the dog die or something?"

"No! No! No! He's leaving me,' cried her um.

"Who? The dog?"

"No, Roger! He's filed for divorce, he sent me the papers, he's suing me!"

"Whoa, whoa, whoa, Mum! Hold the phone a sec, yeah? Dad's doing what?"

Susan gives Harry the letter Roger left her. "Here, read that."

Harriet could hear her Dad's voice as she read the note.

"Dear Susan,
It cannot have escaped your notice that the sexual spark we once shared has long since died. When the children left home, you gave the distinct impression that we would have more time for each other and, specifically, that our sex life would

improve. In actual fact, our sex life has gotten worse than ever. I was even looking forward to some show of affection at my last birthday, but as usual, nothing happened.

Attached are the papers for our divorce. Although I still love you, and always will, I can't go on pretending I am content with our situation. On top of this, for the continuous emotional and personal damage our completely unsatisfactory sex life has caused me, I'm suing you for 'False Promise'. You always say "Tomorrow, tomorrow," but you know it's just a lie. You will be hearing from my solicitor.

> *Your husband,*
> *Roger"*

All Harry could say after reading her father's note was "Bloody hell!"

Whilst Harry was downstairs making her mum a cup of tea and her mum was having a rest, Tom had arrived. Harry and Tom sat at the kitchen table in silence.

"Shit!" said Tom.

"Shit!" replied Harry.

After a while Harry spoke again. "I can't understand it. Dad's such a pussycat. I thought he was happy being retired. He's got his garden and his golf."

"I know what you mean," replied Tom. "I haven't noticed anything. He seemed fine."

"Poor Mum," said Harriet.

"Dad must have gone nuts or something." Tom scratched his head as he re-read his dad's letter. Tom started to laugh.

"What's so funny?" demanded Harry.

"Suing for an unsatisfactory sex life. I can't imagine them having sex."

"Well, logically, they must have had sex at least twice or we wouldn't be here."

Tom nodded his head in agreement.

"But Harry, can you really imagine Mum and Dad getting down and dirty?"

"Oh God Tom, don't. I'm still hungover. Christ! I could do with a fag."

"Do Mum and Dad know you smoke yet?"

"'Course not. Mum would do her nut."

"Probably just as well they don't know that they sent you to business school for three years just to end up working in a Porn Dungeon then, isn't it?"

"It's not a Porn Dungeon. It's an alternative specialist leisure outlet."

"You say alternative specialist leisure outlet, the sign outside says 'Porn Dungeon'."

Suddenly, Susan enters the room, still looking terrible.

"Mum, what are you doing out of bed? Do you want a cup of tea?"

Susan sits down and nods pathetically. She then speaks to Tom. "Have you spoken to your father yet?"

"Yes, I have. He says he's O.K. If you need to get in touch he'll be staying at the Selsdon Park Hotel."

"What?! He's staying at the Selsdon Park Hotel?"

If your stupid bastard of a father thinks he can stay at a five-star hotel taking money out of our joint account, he can bloody well buck his ideas up. I'm getting a new conservatory in the Spring and there is no way in hell that's not going to happen just because your father's got a bloody hard-on!" With that, Susan stormed out, leaving Tom and Harry in stunned silence.

Eventually, Tom spoke, "Did you hear that?"

"Yeah!" said Harry.

Mum won't allow Dad to stay in any hotel, never mind the Selsdon. He obviously can't stay here, so that only leaves him with two options."

Harry becomes mortified as she cottons on to Tom's meaning. "Well, he can't stay at mine. I'm stocktaking at the moment and I'm wall-to-wall with 'Rampant Rabbits'."

"Well, he can't stay at mine either. I don't even have a sofa bed!" replied Tom." Look, there's only one real way we can decide fair and square who Dad stays with." Tom takes a two pound coin out of his pocket and as he tosses it into the air, Harriet calls "Heads!"

Later that evening, with Tom cursing his luck, he and his dad enter Tom's one-bedroom apartment with Tom carrying his dad's suitcase and his duvet.

"Welcome to casa Tom," he said, trying to lighten the mood.

"Where's all the furniture? Have you just moved in?" enquired his dad.

"It's a look, Dad, it's called minimalistic."

"It's certainly that. Where am I going to sleep?"

"Ah, well, I don't actually have a sofa bed at the minute."

"That's alright," replied Roger, making his way into the bedroom, "you'll be O.K. sleeping on the couch, won't you?"

Tom nodded his head miserably, contemplating trying to fit his six-foot frame onto a five-foot settee. Tom then remembers he has not tidied up his bedroom after rushing out that morning to play golf.

"Er, wait a minute, Dad," said Tom trying to stop his father from entering the room ahead of him.

It's too late as Roger surveys the various bits of debris from his son's last encounter with a young lady. He picks up an item of lady's underwear from Tom's bed. "This your girlfriend's?" asks Roger.

Tom nods his head.
"Where's the rest of it?" He then pokes his finger through the hole in a pair of crotchless panties and wiggles it to demonstrate. Tom snatches them away

and tosses them into the corner where there are other items of underwear.

Roger gestures to a pair of handcuffs that hang on the bedpost. "She's a policewoman then?" states Roger.

Desperately trying to change the subject, Tom suggests going for a drink.

"Come on dad we'll sort all this out when we get back."

Meanwhile, that evening, Harry is lounging in her living room wearing a pair of joggers and an old t-shirt. She's chain-smoking and listening to some punk music. Her apartment, even though it is bigger than Tom's, is indeed wall to wall with Rampant Rabbits and a range of other sex toys. She gets up, dodges all the stock that is laying about, and makes herself a cup of tea.

There is a knock on the door. Harry is confused as she is not expecting anyone. She looks out of her kitchen window and sees her mother standing at the door. Urgently, Harry proceeds to waft the cigarette smoke about and looks desperately for somewhere to stub her fag. Eventually, she just grinds it into the leaves of a nearby potted plant. Straightening herself up, she answers the door.

"Mum, hi! What a pleasant surprise."

Susan is more composed now. Her make-up and clothing are, once again, pristine. Her expression has reverted back to that of casual annoyance rather than the mess it had been in earlier. Susan pushes her way passed Harry and into the apartment. She freezes almost immediately and sniffing the air asks, "Have you been smoking, Harriet?"

"No! No! That's Sharon, my roommate."

"I never knew you had a roommate?"

"Yeah! For a while now. You know, helps pay the bills and that."

Before Harry can stop her, Susan marches into the living room. She is surrounded by all sorts of sex toys.

"What on earth are all these things?"
Harry thinks quickly. "Toys! They're toys! Sharon works in a toy shop."

Susan picks up one of the 'toys' and investigates it with puzzled interest. Harry tries to hide her amusement at her mother's bemusement.

"Can't say it's much of a toy, Harriet. I mean what's it supposed to do? Kids will play with anything these days."

"I was just making a cup of tea, Mum, do you want one?" Susan nods her head.

Harry begins making the tea. As she does so, Susan begins to look through her bag and finally produces a large brown envelope. "I received this in the post today"

"Is it about the divorce papers already?" asks Harry.

"No, it's about the other thing, suing me for 'false promise'. It says I have to attend a civil court to defend the petition. I don't know what to do."

Harry thought she was being helpful when she asked her mum, "Have you thought about seeing a solicitor?"

"Harriet, I'll not discuss my sex life with a complete stranger!"

"You'll have to discuss it with someone sooner or later, Mum. Why don't you just talk to Dad? I'm sure he would come right back and pack up this whole silly game if you just got together with him and talked it through."

"But there's nothing to talk about! There's nothing wrong, Harriet. For God's sake, I buy my smalls from Marks & Spencer, that should be enough for any man."

"Your small what?" asks Harry.

"You know, pants and things."

"Mum, what do you wear in bed, specifically?"

'Pyjamas, of course." Susan was starting to look a bit indignant.

"Look Mum, I might be able to help you out on this one."

With that, Harry started to rummage through one of her various boxes in her living room. She finds what she is looking for and plops an Anne Summers catalogue on her mother's lap.

"Why don't you have a glass of wine and have a gander through that? I'm here if you need to ask any questions, O.K.?"

Susan looks puzzled but opens the magazine. Her eyes widen dramatically.

At about the same time in the evening, Tom and his dad sit opposite one another in the latest trendy bar in Croydon. Roger has a pint of bitter whereas Tom is drinking the latest flavoured Gin and Vermouth cocktail.

"Look Dad, you can't keep avoiding the subject all night. What's the crack with you and Mum?"

Roger takes a long pull of his pint before answering. "Son, did you know that man was put on this earth with the ability to copulate, on average, four times a day, every day?"

Tom nods, clearly impressed, even for his track record. Roger continues.

"Even with weekends off, that's twenty times a week, not twenty times a month and certainly not what I'm getting at the moment which is about once a year if I'm lucky. Even then, she never joins in. It's as though she's doing me one almighty favour."

"Oh, come on, Dad, I don't believe that. What about every Saturday afternoon, when we were kids, you and Mum used to go upstairs and lock yourselves in your bedroom for a couple of hours."

"We were watching the Coronation Street omnibus. Don't tell anyone that. Your mum would kill me if the neighbours found out we watched any of the soaps."

Tom goes to laugh but stops when he sees that his dad is not joking.

"You're not kidding, are you?"

Roger shakes his head slowly with a rather sad look on his face.

"You'll find out one day, Tom, that there are few things more painful than constant rejection in the marital bed from the woman who is supposed to love you."

"Have you tried talking to Mum about it, properly like?

"I've tried, Son. Even talked about counselling. But your mother would swallow her own tongue before she admits there's a problem. You know how she can be, she won't ask anyone for help. Too proud."

"Have you, you know, tried to spice things up a bit?"

"What? You mean with handcuffs and crotchless knickers? I bought your mother a black all-in-one for Christmas once. She refused to wear it, said it was 'too tight'. I told her that was the bloody point! Mention the word 'basque' to your mum, and she'll go outside and bloody sunbathe."

They both laugh and sip their drinks before Roger continues. "It's not about how many times we do it, and it's not about what she does or doesn't wear. It's not even about threesomes or whether the dog joins in. I just want us to make love."

Early the next morning, Tom and Harry are sitting outside their local 'greasy spoon'. Tom shivers and looks disapprovingly at Harry smoking.

"We have to sit outside and freeze to death because of your filthy habit. If you hurry up and finish that fag, we can eat breakfast inside. You should think about giving them up, Harry, you know they're bad for you."

"I'll tell you what's bad for me, it's Mum coming round and crying on my shoulder."

"Whoa, hang on. You don't have to put Dad up. He hangs around the place like a lost puppy. He even goes on about missing the dog as he has no one to talk to during the day when I'm at work. What's that about?"

"The only good thing about Mum coming round is that no matter what room we are in, as she is moaning about Dad, she cleans the room as she goes. I've only got to be in the bedroom next time she visits and the whole house will be spotless."

Both son and daughter sit for a while trying to get their thoughts together to suggest a solution.

"Come on sis, you're in the sex industry, you're an expert for God's sake, can't you talk to Mum about it?"

"Well I gave her an Anne Summers catalogue to look through the other day and she nearly started crying. Anyway, how is Dad bearing up?"

"He's adamant he's going to go through the whole procedure. In fact, he's made an appointment with his solicitor this morning."

***

Sam Connery, Roger's solicitor and old school friend, was dreading the appointment with Roger. Sam was good at his job. You could see he was successful by the cut of suit and the expensive Rolex watch on his wrist. Not used to losing, he was reluctant to take Roger's case on.

He had spent a couple of hours the previous evening searching the internet to see if anybody had been successful in trying to sue their spouse for bedroom 'False Promise' but to no avail. He had been successful, in the past, dealing with Breach of Contract but he could see no way he could use the same arguments, in front of a judge, to plead Roger's case.

After Sam's secretary brought Roger into his office and they both went through the usual pleasantries, Sam sat back in his chair and got straight to the point. "I was up until midnight last night researching past cases and, to be perfectly honest, I have never heard of anybody being sued for false promise connected to their sex lives. The lack of sex will be useful when we come to argue the divorce proceedings but, as your solicitor, you've got no chance claiming emotional distress, or whatever, when it comes to matters of the marital bed. If it's any consolation, I'm confident I can get you a good financial settlement from the divorce, but that's all."

"I'm not that interested in the money," replied Roger

"Roger, if I had a pound coin for every time I've heard that in this office I would be living in the Bahamas. Funnily enough, though, with you, I actually believe it. Are you willing to waste your retirement money on a case you will most likely lose? I don't do discounts, not even for old school chums like you."

"I know, Sam, but if this is what it takes to make my wife sit up and take notice of me, then it is what I'll do."

"It seems a lot of money for a bit of attention." Roger sat contemplating the advice. "If I told you, Sam, that Susan and I once made passionate love on the kitchen table after a game of strip poker, would you believe me? Well we did, Sam, and it doesn't seem that long ago to be honest. These days, I'm lucky to get a mad passionate conversation about conservatories."

"O.K., Roger, I see your point. But when she married you, she promised to love, honour and obey, that doesn't say anything about her shagging you twice nightly."

"Well, surely sex comes under the heading of 'love', doesn't it?"

"Rog, Rog, Rog. It's not like it was in our day, mate. Men don't meet a girl, go out with her, and then get married. These days, sex isn't about love. It's the inter-gender equivalent of going down the pub for a couple of pints. It's a hobby, not a prerequisite to having children. Sex and love are two different things so we can chuck that argument out of the window straight away."

"I don't think so, Sam. I think you're wrong."

"Wrong or right, it's what stands up in court that matters."

That evening, Susan knocks on Harry's door in what is becoming something of a ritual. This time, Harry's not waiting in a room that needs cleaning. She answers the door dressed like a tarty version of a policewoman.

"Why are you dressed like that?" Susan asks.

"Come in Mum, come in."

Bewildered, Susan enters Harry's flat. A glass of wine is pushed into her hand by her daughter who, at the same time, refreshes her own glass with the bottle.

"What's going on?" asks Susan.

"We're going out for dinner. It's my friend Sheila's hen night so we thought we would start the celebrations early."

Susan looks down at the glass of wine in her hand. "I'm in no mood for a party. I have other things to worry about."

"That's exactly why we're going out. A night on the town is what you need to cheer you up."

"Well, where are we going?"

"Just to a restaurant, Mum."

"O.K. If it's just a restaurant."

"Great! Here, put this on."

Harry hands her mum a policewoman's hat.

"Put it on, it's fancy dress tonight. We can go as those two police woman on the telly - Scott and Bailey."

Meanwhile Tom and Roger are heading down to the pub to meet with a few of Tom's mate. Tom had sorted his dad out with a smart pair of Chinos and a really nice shirt which, secretly, Roger thought he looked the part in.

The hen party had descended on Sheila's house and it was decided that a few more drinks would be the order of the day before they moved on to the restaurant.

Harry introduces her mum to all of her mates and Sheila, the bride-to-be, is dressed as a schoolgirl. She had her arm around Susan telling her she couldn't wait to get married to her lovely fiancée but she was determined to have one last night of freedom.

The room had a smoky atmosphere and was filled with tacky party decorations and half-full spirit bottles. The hen party consisted of women of various ages who were all drinking and clearly enjoying themselves. All of them were in fancy dress as either nurses, police officers, or other hen night cliches. Sheila stood out dressed all in white sexy underwear with a couple of car 'L' plates hanging from around her neck.

When asked what she wanted to drink, she answered she would prefer a sweet sherry. Sheila just laughed and mixed Susan a cocktail.

"Mmm, that's actually quite nice," Susan remarked. "What's it called?'

"I call it the 'Mind-Blowing Orgasm," replied Sheila.

Meanwhile, Roger and Tom have ended up in a trendy bar along with three of Tom's mates - Mark, Jason and John. The bar is full of young men, all with trendy haircuts, similar voices and jobs in the city.

"Tom's old man, eh! Bet he's a chip off the old block, then?" Jason asked.

"I'd like to think he is," replied Roger.

"Bet you have trouble keeping up with all of his girlfriends?" Jason gave Roger a gentle prod in the ribs and a conciliatory wink.

"Actually, he never brings them round." replied Roger.

Tom hastily changed the subject.

"Come on Jase, it's your round."

"What does everyone want then, the usual?"

"Can I just have a pint Of Bitter please?"

"Dad, they don't do pints here, just cocktails and shots."

Jason returns with a tray of drinks. The drinks consist of bottles of Alcopops and several small, but lethal, glasses of shots.

"Brain Dead!" they all cry, downing their shots in one go. Roger steels himself and follows suit.

"Wow! That's got some kick in it, what the hell's in it?"

They all laugh at Roger's naivety and quickly order another round.

Later that evening after they had left the restaurant, the local karaoke bar is packed and up on the stage in an obvious stage of inebriation are Sheila, Harry and rather reluctantly, Susan. She is clearly not used to being on stage but is starting to feel the effects of the consumed cocktails and is joining in with the chorus to 'I Will Survive'. The hen party is now noticeably drunker and noisier and shout encouragement to the three singers on stage.

Coming off stage, Harry says, "That was great, Mum, I never knew you could dance or sing?"

"I used to do Drama at Secondary School. I had quite a love for the stage."

Suddenly, the hen night is interrupted by a handsome man in a policeman's uniform.

The music in the karaoke bar stops and the man addresses Sheila. "Excuse me, madam, are you Sheila Brown?"

"Yes, that's me." replies Sheila.

All of a sudden, the song 'Macho Man' begins to play and the man in the police uniform begins to strip, much to the amusement of the collective hen party.

Susan is shocked, but intrigued by the display and with the cajoling of Harry, gradually begins to enjoy it more and more, eventually taking her turn dancing with the stripper. For the coup de grace, the stripper removes his G-string, revealing his 'goods' to the assembled party, who begin to cheer and applaud, bar Susan, who gasps and says to Harry in astonishment,

"My husbands is bigger than that!"

All of the hen party crack up laughing at this and the stripper, who is now getting dressed and looks annoyed.

As the night continues, Roger starts to look a little worse for wear. "Where are we going now? I want to go home. I've got to be in court in the morning."

Tom's having none of it. "Come on, Dad, one for the road at a little club I know."

Roger doesn't realise, but they are heading to a neon sign that bears the legend 'G-Spot Gentleman's Club.' They enter into the dark and dingy strip club, where loud music and pole dancers feature predominately. Sitting by the stage with fresh drinks in their hands are Tom, Roger and the rest of the lads. They cheer and whistle, all except Roger, who merely gazes upwards, awestruck, as the exotic dancer strips and gyrates to the loud music.

"What do think then, Dad, makes a change from golf, eh?!"

Roger remains awestruck and paralysed as a pink, feathered boa is flung onto his shoulder by the dancer.

Outside the karaoke bar, Susan and Harry hug as Susan has decided she has had enough and Harry and the girls are going on to a nightclub.

"I haven't had so much fun in years," says Susan.

"You could join us going to the nightclub. It's brilliant and it's open until 5am."

"Far too late for me, I'm afraid. I'll be fine and thanks for tonight, Harry. I had a really good time, but I have to be up early in the morning ready for the court case."

At the end of their night out, Tom, Roger and Tom's friends stagger out of the strip club. Roger is supported by Tom and Jason, who are, in turn, flanked by John and Mark. They all look slightly ill, tired and very drunk. Roger still wears the pink feathered boa around his shoulders.

"Well that was bloody incredible, but I really think we should go home now."

"Dad, we can't go home until we find a kebab shop, it's the law." There was a general murmur of enthusiasm from the lads to this suggestion.

"Kebab! I haven't had a kebab for twenty years!"

"Twenty years without a kebab?" Jason was astonished. "What did you eat when you were drunk?"

"I don't get drunk anymore. My wife and I used to go out all the time. Not anymore. How I wish she was here."

"Don't worry, Dad. You and Mum will work it out somehow. But right now, I think we should all worry about where the nearest kebab shop is."

Even though it is three o'clock in the morning, Susan finds it difficult to sleep as she is worried about the court case and what she should wear. That gives her an idea. She gets out of bed and picks up her police woman's hat. Then, as though she has made up her mind about something, she picks up her mobile and dials Harriet's number.

Its four o'clock in the morning before Roger slumps into his bed. He looks the worse for wear. He screws up his kebab wrapper, throws it at the bin near to the toilet door and misses. He looks at the pink feathered boa disdainfully and casts it aside. He picks up his mobile phone and switches it to camera mode. He presses the 'selfie' button to reveal his drunken features on the screen.
With no dog to speak to he talks to himself. "The disco's gave way to dinner parties. The dinner parties gave way to 'afternoon teas'. What comes

next? What do you do when nothing is fun anymore? When you're best friend is a stranger who shares your bed? I wonder how the case will go? I'm sure you can sue for anything nowadays. Can you sue for bedroom neglect? Emotional, as well as physical. I hope I can sue because the spark has definitely gone out of our relationship and I'm sure there is no chance of it coming back. You can't charge a dud battery. I'll just have to get another one."

Rodger looked closer at his drink-ravaged face. "With those looks, mate, you've got no chance in the pulling department." He laughed to himself, switched off his phone, and turned over in bed determined to get some sleep before the big day.

The following morning in the annex to the civil courtroom, Roger's solicitor is giving his last minute pep talk.

"Basically, I'll just tell the judge what you have already told me. I'll lay it on thick and give him the old sob story about your rejection etc. Actually, all the facts give you good grounds for divorce but, and I have to emphasize this to you, this is your last chance to pull out of the 'false promise' angle."

Tom, who was there supporting his dad, added, "It's not too late. You and Mum could still talk this over, couldn't you?"

At the other end of the annex enters Susan, Harry and Susan's solicitor, Emma Forbes, a prim and proper-looking woman who is very serious and is all about the business of the day. Susan looks completely different to what she usually looks like. She is wearing her blonde hair down onto her shoulders and her make-up is complete with dark red lipstick giving her a rather sultry look. A long, fashionable coat and high heels complete this very different look.

Emma is giving Susan one last briefing.

"I think the chances of this case swinging in our favour are excellent. I think the 'false promise' angle can be used to our advantage. As Mr. Hastings is retired and you are still working in a highly-paid job, we can say Roger is only after your money rather than legitimate compensation for what the judge will agree is a ridiculous accusation."

"Roger's not like that. Money's never been an issue between us."

Emma turned and took hold of Susan's arm. "The point is we should be able to reduce the damage of the divorce settlement if we play our cards right."

Harry is holding her mum's hand and is clearly worried. "Are you sure you know what you're doing, Mum?"

"Relax, Harry, it'll be fine. I have everything under control."

At this comment, Harry looked quizzically at her mother, not knowing what she meant.

At the other end of the annex, Roger, Tom and Sam continue their way across the hall.

"So let's go through the facts again, Roger. You financially supported your wife through her lengthy period of training in the early years of her career to get her qualifications, yes?"

Roger nodded, wondering where Sam was going with this.

"Score one. You can confirm, without fear of contradiction, that your sex life has been practically non-existent for a number of years?"

"I think so, yes," replied Roger.

"Score two. And finally, is there any way you can prove, beyond a shadow of doubt, that Susan, verbally or otherwise, promised, and I do mean promised, that your sex life would improve once your kids left home?"

"Not promised exactly. Suggested, certainly."

"Oh, well. Two out of three isn't bad."

Meanwhile, Susan, Harry and Emma continue their progress with Emma still asking the questions.

"Just as a bit of back-up, can you think of any time when your husband might have suggested, or demanded, anything you might deem as an unusual request?"

"I'm sorry, I don't know what you mean?"

"You know, whips, animals, lesbian threesome, watching from a closet while you have sex with another man?"

Harry put her hands over her face as she didn't want her mum to know she was cracking up laughing.

"Certainly not!" replied an affronted Susan.

Emma raised both of her hands. "I'm just checking, that's all, just checking."

Both parties were then called into the civil courtroom. They sit facing the judge who is concentrating on reviewing the case notes. Roger, Tom and Sam sit on one side of the room whilst Susan, Harry and Emma sit on the other. The judge does not acknowledge their presence but starts shaking his head slowly from side-to-side and the only noise to be heard in the room is the judge tutting at what he is reading. Roger and Susan exchange glances.

"I actually don't believe what I'm reading. It seems to me that two intelligent adults could have sorted their differences long before deciding to come to a court of law."

Sam and Emma both start to speak but the judge holds his hand up to stop them from interrupting him.

"I have to ask," the judge continued addressing both Roger and Susan, "if you would like to take some time to discuss this privately so that you might reach an amicable decision without the courts intervention."

Roger and Susan look at each other and nod their consent.

"Very well, please retire to the privacy of the chambers."

Roger and Susan enter the room and stand at opposite ends of a table.

"You look lovely today, have you done something to your hair? And is that a new coat?"

"Yes, I bought it especially for today."

"It's very n..." Roger is cut short as Susan lets the coat drop to the floor, revealing a full set of expensive lingerie underneath.

"Bloody hell!" exclaimed Roger.

Susan also holds up a set of love beads from Harry's shop.

"Apparently, we can have a lot of fun walking around Sainsbury's with these."

"I think we can leave the shopping until later." They both move towards each other and kiss passionately.

Back in the courtroom, everyone is waiting patiently for Roger and Susan to come out of the chambers. Tom and Harry lean over to one another. "What do you think is taking them so long?" asks Tom. "I hope they're O.K."

"I wouldn't worry too much," Harry replied with a knowing look on her face.

Faintly, in the silence of the courtroom, there can be heard the moans and cries of pleasure from Roger and Susan.

Tom grins, while the judge looks affronted.

Tom stands up to address the courtroom. "You know, I think everything is going to be O.K. now."

When Roger and Susan finally come back into the Annex looking rather sheepish, Tom started clapping, then Harriet, and soon the whole courtroom joined in, even the judge.

Roger gave a theatrical bow. Susan joined in with an extravagant curtsy and everyone laughed with relief. Rog and Sue were back.

The Tennis Match

Bill Richmond was fifty-two years old, with a fifty-two inch waistline to match. Success had come to him late in life. He had joined a builder's yard straight from school and had spent twenty years learning the trade from the ground up. It was not until Bill's father died and left him his home that Bill decided to branch out on his own as a property developer. The ex-council house was renovated and sold, and with the money earned, he built two semi-detached houses. He had worked hard and he had worked well, and with a little help from the '80s property boom, he had done very nicely for himself, thank you.

One of the perks of his success was the brand new Range Rover that served as his company car. It was luxurious, spacious and, essential on this sweltering summer morning, fully air-conditioned. He had done his time sweating like a pig in a scrapheap white van and frankly, he did not miss it.

The car phone rang and he pressed a pudgy digit to the hands-free kit.

"Hello, Bill Richmond."

"Hi, Bill. Jim Smith."

"Ah, Jim! You must be ringing to tell me you've sold number twenty-two?"

Jim laughed, his voice tinny on the car speakers. "Given I only put the for sale board up two days ago, I think that's unlikely, mate. I'm good, but I'm not that good." Jim was a senior partner at a local estate agents, and the man who handled most of Bill's property sales.

Bill chuckled. "Go on then. If it's not good news then it must be bad."

"Far from it," said Jim. "I've got a tip for you, something you might be interested in."

"Oh, yeah?"

"You've heard of Brian Thomas Electrics? Clover Court?"

Bill thought, recalling a thin man with a bushy mustache stood behind the counter of a jumble sale shop of second-hand electronics. "Yes, I know it."

"Well, he's on his way out."

"Way out?"

"Stomach cancer. Not long left, so I'm told."

Bill winced and briefly yearned for a fonder time when cancer was something that happened to the distant or the elderly. These days, it seemed to be keeping closer company; acquaintances, friends, old faces - the vague immortals from his youth bought into dreadful immediacy. On colder nights, it sometimes felt like a hand upon the shoulder.

"Poor sod," was all he could think of to say.

"Yeah, well," said Jim, distracted. "Turns out there could be a real earner in this one. I've had one of his kids on the phone already pricing up the old shop and the flat above. I've looked into it. It's a solid estate, good ground. Needs a lot of work, but for the right man..."

"Meaning me."

"Meaning you. The son wants this sold up and out of his hair as quickly as possible. Can't wait to get his hands on a bit of cash, I should think."

And you can't wait to get your hands on a bit of commission, thought Bill, but he didn't say so. Business was business, even where death was concerned. In fact, it occurred to him the amount of quick sales of dead relative's homes he handled - old photographs left behind, a mug, a keepsake. Things forgotten, and quickly gotten rid of.

At least in those instances the body was cold, he thought, *and not, in fact, still living.*

"Can I get in to have a look at it?"

"Yeah, anytime you like," said Jim. "The old man's got home help, so there's somebody there 'round the clock."

"Home help?"

"Yeah, you know. They make sure he's comfortable."

"He's not in hospital?"

"Nah, home help."

Bill thought for a moment. He was pricing up a dead man's home while the dead man still lived there. Did it feel wrong? Should it feel wrong?

"Bill?"

"Yeah, I'll drop in. I'll go later this morning, let you know my thoughts on the valuation."

"Great, I'll phone ahead and let…"

Bill didn't wait for Jim to finish, but clicked the button to hang-up. He did not know this fat, rich builder in his shining, showroom utility vehicle, why he should feel so bleak? A summers day, with air-conditioning no less. A faithful wife, children he had got on with better since they had gone their own way, one to university, one to an accountancy firm. And still...

His morning went quickly, forms and figures and signing on dotted lines, and it was half an hour before lunch when he once more squeezed his bulk into the Range Rover and made his way to Clover Court.

He knocked on the door of a rundown shop, a place which specialized in repairing household appliances, back when people still repaired household appliances. He knocked again, and was answered by the home help, a thin but jovial lady who could have been fifty or sixty. Or seventy, or who knows. He wondered where they came from, these eternal matrons, these dressed-down Valkyries. He wondered if they would come for him one day, when he was pale and wasted, pajama-clad and reeking of fear.

She offered him tea and he accepted, taking time while the kettle boiled to wander around the property. He had already made up his mind that the garages at the rear could be knocked down, making way for a light industrial unit. The showroom at front could easily accommodate a bookies and an off-license, both safe bets in this area of town. If he bought at the right price, and quick sales almost always came at the right price, then he could stand to make a hefty profit. Jim Smith had been right, it could be a real earner.

Later, he sipped his tea and smiled politely while the home help chatted in a sing-song tone, and soon enough he made his excuses and prepared to leave.

"The upstairs?" said the home help. "The living accommodation, didn't you want to see it?"

Bill felt a cold clenching in his guts. He did not want to see it. But business was business, even where death was concerned. "Thanks for reminding me," he said, and turned a boney smile.

He made his way upstairs. It did not bother him that there was linoleum on the floor, or that the bath taps were leaking badly or that the living room was sparsely furnished. These were easily mended, ripped away and discarded, making way for the new, the shiny, the As Seen On TV products.

He opened a door, revealing a front bedroom. "Good size," he mumbled.

He opened another door and stopped. There was a muggy smell of sleep and blanket, of breath after breath. The room was dim, curtains closed against the sun. A figure lay in the dark, cocooned in his bed, mummified in sleep. Bill started as the home help appeared at his side like a butler in a cartoon comedy.

"I'm sorry," he said awkwardly. "I wasn't thinking."

"It's quite alright," the home help smiled, skin wrinkling around gentle eyes. "You haven't woken him. If truth be told, it takes quite a lot to wake him once he does go down. Besides," she added, "Brian wouldn't have minded anyway. He always enjoyed company."

"You knew him, then?" said Bill. "Before he was..." he searched for the right words, found nothing good. "before he was ill?"

"Oh, yes," said the home help. "I'm Gladys Turner. I was Brian's mixed doubles partner."

"Mixed doubles?" echoed Bill, bemused.

"Tennis." Gladys smiled again. "Brian and I played for the Highgrove first team, many years ago, of course. Look..." The old woman picked up a framed photograph that was on the bedside table. It was the only photograph in the room. "If you look closely, I'm the young lady standing on the far left of the picture. I was a brunette in those days." She raised a hand unconsciously to her shoulder, fiddling for locks that were no longer there.

Bill looked at the team photograph. Stern young faces on bodies dressed all in white, apart from a sharp-faced girl in a blue top with red and yellow piping on the sleeves. "Who's this girl here?" he asked.

Gladys laughed. "That's no girl!" she said. "This was the swinging sixties, young man. Brian had beautiful long hair. This was taken on his sixteenth birthday."

"This was some sort of party then?"

"No, much more important than that. This was the day of the club's men's singles final. No one as young as Brian had ever reached the final before. See the man standing next to him?"

Bill looked at the older man, rigidly straight under his thinning hair, immaculate in his traditional whites. "Is that his dad?"

"Don't be silly," said Gladys, gently prodding Bill's protruding stomach. "That's Henry Jones. Club Captain." The old lady sighed and, picture still in hand, began walking toward the door. Bill followed her as she talked, almost to herself. "Nowadays tennis centers have swimming pools and restaurants and a crèche for the kiddies, but in the '60s, you had your six shale courts, a wooden pavilion to get changed in, and if you had to pee, you either played on with your legs crossed or slipped behind the hedges when no one was looking."

They walked into the small but serviceable kitchen. "Would you like another cup of tea, young man?"

Bill found that he did, and said as much. The kettle was filled, and clicked on to boil.

Gladys cleared her throat. "That was a special day," she said. "Most of our club matches were played during the week, in the evenings, and Saturday afternoons were normally reserved for friendlies between the members. Not the day of young Brian Thomas's sixteenth birthday, though. That was the day of the men's singles championship competition, and the youngest member was going up against the club captain, a man who'd won the championship four years in a row."

Gladys looked out of the window, her pale eyes seeing something other than a rundown forecourt and a row of shabby council houses. "It was a gorgeous day. Perfect weather for tennis, not a cloud in the sky. Everybody from the club had come to watch, most of them brought their families. A gorgeous day."

As Gladys talked, Bill sipped at his tea, trying to consolidate, in his mind, the brightly dressed boy in the photograph and the broken man lying in the next room.

***

The day of the men's final tennis match at Crawley Tennis Club was a beautiful day, ideal for the top sporting event in the club's calendar that year. The sky was blue, and only enough wind to make the change of ends on the tennis court a possibly change of tactics for either player.

Coincidentally, it was with excitement that Brian Thompson unwrapped his sixteenth birthday present after breakfast with his mum, dad and younger brother, Billy, looking on. It was a brand new set of tennis kit. T-Shirt, shorts, socks and a pair of Green Flash Dunlop tennis shoes. Brian was gobsmacked.

"Well, we've got to have you looking the part today of all days," said his mum affectionately.

"There's also this," said his dad as he handed Brian a brand new Wilson tennis racket.

"Can I have your old one?!" shouted Billy.

Brian was in tears when he hugged his mum and dad. He could not believe how lucky he was and it went a long way to helping him with his confidence ahead of the men's final that afternoon.

Brian's dad drove the family the two miles to the tennis club in his gleaming Woseley 15/60, his pride and joy. When Brian got out of the car, he was surprised to see that so many people had turn up to watch the game. He spotted Gladys Turner, his mixed doubles partner, in the crowd and gave her what he hoped was a confident wave.

As Brian approached the court, his opponent, Henry Jones, called out, "Come on young Thompson, we haven't got all day you know."

As with all the finals, the club would ask another member if they would be good enough to sit in the umpire's chair and officiate the game. Brian was a bit puzzled when he saw it was Frank Smith, Jones' doubles partner, who was sitting high in the chair.

"Ah well, hopefully he'll be fair-minded in his decisions," thought the young lad.

This was immediately dispelled when the umpire announced, "Jones has won the toss and elected to serve."

Brian had not even been asked whether he wanted 'rough' or 'smooth', the traditional way of deciding who would serve first, or if they preferred, which end would they want to start from depending on the wind and the angle of the sun.

Brian was shocked even further when Smith said "Play" and before the youngster had his bearings, Jones had sent down an unplayable serve. "Ace, fifteen love," stated the umpire. They had not even warmed up, giving Brian a chance to 'get his eye in'. Brian walked quickly to the other side of the court determined to be ready for the next point. He just managed to get his racket to the ball with his backhand but the ball flew into the net. Before he knew it, he was one nil down and they were changing ends.

Brian grabbed a mouthful of water from his bottle only to hear Jones asking "What time are we meeting up tonight for a drink, old boy?"

"Well, this match isn't going to last very long, is it? We can grab a snifter in the clubhouse before we need to go and get changed."

It was Brian's turn to serve. His nerves had not quite settled and his first efforts resulted in a double fault. Love fifteen down. He made a better fist of his next first serve only for Jones to smash a forehand winner down the line. Love thirty. Two more double faults gave the game to Jones who held his serve to make it three love in games to him.

Brian took the opportunity of the change-over to try and think what was wrong. He had to get over being intimidated by Jones and Smith and just try to play his own game. Things got a little better but before long, Jones had won the first set six games to one.

Brian tried to look on the bright side. He had won one game. How did he do it? He noticed that although Jones had a big serve and a good forehand, his backhand was his weakest shot.

"Well then," thought Brian, *"I'll concentrate on playing to his backhand."*

The tactic proved useful as the next six games went with serve. Three all, time for Brian to serve again. He constantly rallied to Jones's backhand and won his serve 40-30 and for the first time that day, he had drawn level. He had won the vital seventh game and now the pressure was on Jones. The crowd was getting more involved as they could sense there may be an upset on the cards. There was some disgruntled boos and hisses when Smith, the umpire, declared a winning forehand of Brian's to be out when everybody, including Jones, could see it was clearly inside the line. Instead of Jones doing the gentlemanly thing and overrule the mistake, he said nothing and Brian lost the game. It was now four games each in the second set with all to play for. Two more winning games for Jones and it would all be over for the youngster.

Brian was serving a lot better now. His nerves were gone and he was enjoying the thrill of hitting well-placed tennis shots. Unfortunately, when he was 40-0 up on his serve and ready to take a 5-4 lead, he mis-hit a forehand. The ball went straight at

Jones and hit him smack in the testicles. Jones went down like a sack of spuds.

Smith jumped off the umpire's chair, snarling at Brian and trying to tend to his friend who was clutching his crown jewels obviously in a lot of pain. To make matters worse, one or two of the crowd started to giggle which did not help matters at all. Brian went around the net and held his hand out to assist Jones to his feet, only to have his hand brushed away.

"My point, umpire, foul play," said Jones. He would have gotten away with it but for Gladys storming onto the court.

"The young lad didn't intend to hit you. It was an unfortunate mis-hit and besides, your body got in the way of a winning shot, so the rules of the game clearly state that you lose the point."

There were murmurs of agreement from the crowd so Smith was unable to do anything except call out the score, "5-4 games to Thompson."

Jones would tell everybody that day, and to this day, that it was the injury to his testicles that lost him his service game and also the second set. One set all.

Brian, by this time, was flying. He had an all-round game with no weaknesses. He started to serve and volley, hitting the volleys deep so they were un-returnable. Henry Jones had no answer to the lad's speed around the court. Jones tried to drop shot Brian but the young lad's fitness was like that of a gazelle around the court and he got to everything

Jones could throw at him. The young lad's all-round game finally got the better of the older man in the three set match and Smith finally had to reluctantly state the end score, "Thompson wins 1-6, 6-4 6-0."

The crowd applauded. Mum, Dad and Billy ran onto the court to congratulate their son and Gladys proudly presented Brian, at the age of sixteen, with the Men's Final Trophy.

***

It was sometime later when Bill Richmond, on his way to one of his building sites, decided to call in at Brian Thompson Electrical as he had heard nothing from the estate agent about whether the property was going to be sold or not.

As he was approaching the shop, he had seen two young lads struggling to carry a large fridge freezer into the back of the company van. As he walked passed them, he said cheerily, "Good Morning" only to receive a couple of sullen stares in reply. He entered the shop and, whilst he was waiting for the shop assistant to appear, he picked up a trophy that stood, pride of place, next to the till. He looked down at the names and stopped at 1968 Brian Thompson, Men's Singles Champion.

Gladys appeared and seeing Bill studying the trophy, said, "I'm glad I kept it. I asked his two sons what they wanted to do with Brian's trophies after his death and all I got in reply was "Throw them in the skip," but I decided to keep this one as it has so many memories about the Tennis Club which, sadly, is no longer there. Children of today just want to play computer games apparently."

"Yes, they struggle with anything physical," said Bill pointing at the two boys finishing loading their van for deliveries.

"Why didn't Brian sell the property then?" asked Bill.

"I assume he decided to leave it to his two sons."

"No," replied Gladys, "Brian left everything to me. The two boys now work for me."

Bill laughed, "I wondered why they looked so miserable."

Bill said his goodbyes and got back into his Range Rover.

He drove away with a smile on his face thinking of a young lad, aged only sixteen, winning the match of his life, with a gleaming trophy to bring back the memories of his achievement.

The Final Sunset

Hunstanton is a holiday resort on the east coast of England overlooking 'The Wash' which is a stretch of water leading into the docks of King's Lynn. Because of its position, it has the unusual feature of actually facing west. One of the main attractions for the many visitors to the town is to park up near the Old Lighthouse on the cliffs and watch some spectacular sunsets.

John looked out on the shimmering stretch of water that was 'The Wash'. Five hundred years earlier, the young King of Norway had stormed the very same cliffs on which John was standing to claim the crown of East Anglia.

It was a place John loved and knew well and with his feet apart and his hands stretched upwards and outwards, so he could put his hands through the large black iron rings that sailors of old used to hoist their cargo from the ships using thick heavy ropes in days gone by. He waited for the end of the day. It was at the bottom of the sixty foot chalk cliffs where smugglers were caught and imprisoned in the cellar room.

The Old Lighthouse dominated the skyline above the waves of the incoming tide. The water was already lapping round John's ankles but he was determined to see one final sunset. It was ten years ago when John's ex-wife Susan told him about Hunstanton having an unusual curvature of the land on which you could actually drive there and watch the sun go down over the water. That weekend, they had promptly popped the two kids, Henry and Elizabeth, into the car and, sharing a picnic, sat on the cliffs of Hunstanton, next to the Old Lighthouse and watched their first beautiful sunset together.

That first trip was followed by another before the decision was made to buy a holiday caravan and, although the caravan park was in what was called New Hunstanton, the favourite part of the day was to walk along the clifftops and watch the sunsets. These three mile walks also proved to be excellent exercise for the family dog, a large black pedigree poodle aptly called 'Lighthouse' who preferred racing along the beach at the foot of the cliffs, running in and out of the sand dunes and small wooden beach houses looking for scraps of picnics left by the thousands of holidaymakers who descended onto the beach on a daily basis.

John's favourite time to come down to the caravan was in winter when the beach was deserted and he could walk along the beach alone, with his dog, and not see another person for hours. His trips to the caravan alone with his dog became more frequent as his marriage slowly went the way of so many others. Boredom had set in, and sex was the occasional duty extended on a Sunday morning before he cut the grass at home as a sort of advance payment. John and Susan rarely talked and both privately-educated children were now at university, both vowing they would have more interesting lives than their 'stuck in the mud' parents.

But then, on one of John's short trips to the caravan, it all changed for him. It was a simple meeting, a chance encounter. She was tall, with very long jet black hair, and she smiled at John one morning as they crossed paths on the clifftops, him walking his poodle and her walking her Alsatian. They had stopped as both dogs went through the ritual of sniffing each other. John said what a lovely Alsatian it was and the stranger just made eye contact, smiled, and went on her way.

John could not sleep that night thinking of her and made a conscious effort to go for his early morning walk at the same time in the hope of bumping into her again. He was to be disappointed that morning but was surprised to bump into her at the local shop later as he was queuing for his morning paper. She was behind him in the queue.

"Hello," he said. She nodded.

"Have you walked your dog this morning yet?" he asked.

"No," she laughed, "not yet."

"Perhaps I'll see you later then," he said.

John had to wait an hour sitting on a bench on top of the cliffs before she appeared. He put the dog lead around his poodle's neck, stood and started to walk with her. John had never met anyone like her. Her eyes seemed to be permanently on fire, her smile danced on her lips, as they walked for miles talking and getting to know each other.

Within minutes, John learned that she was divorced and, astonishingly, John stated out loud that he was going to separate from his wife, Susan, something he had only previously thought about in his own private moments.

They made their way down to the cliff steps to walk back along the beach so that both dogs, let off their leads, could roam free. Her name was Lynda. She was an advertising manager for a local radio station in nearby King's Lynn, she had no children and she enjoyed being single.

"Do you fancy a coffee?" she asked when they reached the sand dunes where the beach huts were situated.

"Fabulous," said John. "There's a cafe near to the Old Lighthouse.

"That's alright," said Lynda, "this is my own private beach hut. I use it as a bolt-hole when work starts to get on top of me."

With that, she turned and approached a cute little beach hut with a small veranda, tied her dog outside, and motioned to John to do the same with his poodle, before they went inside.

John looked around at the furniture, a sofa bed, an acoustic guitar hanging from the wall, matching curtains and cushions, and fashionable straw matting for the floor covering.

"You've got this place looking great," said John turning around to the small kitchenette area where he thought Lynda was making coffee. He was wrong she hadn't been making coffee. She had been getting undressed.

"Don't look so shocked," she said as she stood there dressed in a sexy black bra trying vainly to contain a stunning pair of breasts, and with a matching black G-string just covering her vagina. John's jaw completely dropped in astonishment.

"I want to get to know you better but first we have to find out if we're sexually compatible. It's the most important aspect of a relationship, don't you agree?"

At that moment, John would have agreed that the moon was made of green cheese and he could only gawp as Lynda placed her hands behind her back to release the straps of her bra. The resulting collision of passion was something he had never experienced before and, rather embarrassingly, he orgasmed straight away.

"Don't worry," said Lynda, "lie down on the sofa bed and do as you're told."

John was naked and he was wondering what she was going to do next. He was astonished when she opened a drawer next to the sofa bed full of sex toys he had previously only seen in magazines. John could not believe it when Lynda proceeded to tie his ankles wide apart to the legs of the sofa bed and handcuff his hands, one to the handle of the window and the other to a big iron hook on which several sharp kitchen knives hung down.

When Lynda put her head down to take his penis into her mouth, John initially arched his back and responded instantly. His wife Susan had never done anything like this. When she was satisfied with the hardness, Lynda mounted him, riding him like a frenzied wild stallion. Lynda's black hair went from side-to-side. She continued riding him until she screamed with ecstasy. She collapsed onto John and she did not release him from his handcuffs until she repeated the whole process one more time.

John divorced Susan three months later and moved in with Lynda in King's Lynn. The only question from his children was whether he was still going to financially support them through university. He said he would and they were both fine. Unfortunately, however, his mother and father were not happy about the situation. They could not understand how he could leave Susan who had been a wonderful mother to their grandchildren. This new woman wore red lipstick, for heaven's sake!

His sister had been a little more forthright. "She's a friggin' tart, John. What are you thinking?"

They had not spoken since. The only one who supported him through all of this was his younger brother, Richard.

"You lucky old bugger!" had been his response when John had shown him a picture of Lynda. John beamed with pride as they had always been best mates and he was chuffed when Richard added, "Doesn't look a bit like Susan, does she?"

Richard and John had always shared a love of dogs and Richard actually bred poodles as a hobby. From his first litter, John had kept 'Lighthouse' and

Richard had a male black standard poodle, a beautiful pedigree example named 'Focus'. Richard had an unusual habit of naming his dog after whatever car he was driving at the time.

John was still standing at the foot of the cliffs waiting for the sunset. Whilst he was remembering all of these things, he felt his face burning from the sun and his muscles of his arms were wrenching terribly from being outstretched for so long. The tide was now up to his knees.

Despite most of John's family disapproving of his new relationship, the fact that Richard got on so well with Lynda, when they finally met, meant a lot to John. Over a period of time, he was sure the rest of the family would come to like her as well.

The waves from the incoming tide were now up to John's waist without him noticing as he was lost in thought.

This last year had been the best yet. John had never been happier. Life with Lynda was one big social occasion. Through her media contacts, they went to all the right functions, met the right people and had a fabulous week in Mauritius when Lynda won a Media Sales Award presented by none other than Graham Norton at the International Television and Radio Annual Dinner at the Savoy in London.

Lynda had taken John on a trip around Soho that night to visit several sex shops and buy some more 'toys' to keep by their bed. Lynda was always coming up with something new and exciting for them to try. They had not been to Hunstanton for

ages so when Lynda announced she had to go to
London for a few days on business, John, after
spending the morning pottering about, thought on
the spur of the moment how nice it would be to take
the dog to Hunstanton and enjoy a walk along the
beach once more and hopefully witness yet another
fabulous sunset.

The water was now up to John's chest.

'Lighthouse' bounded out of the car when
John parked on the road next to the clifftops. The
dog recognised their favourite walk and barked with
delight.

"Alright," said John, "we'll go down onto the
beach."

It was another beautiful summer day with the
sun just starting its descent in a clear, cloudless sky
as John enjoyed his walk along the narrow stretch
of beach which had left only moments before the
oncoming tide covered it completely. Only the
rocks and the cliffs would stop it as it had been
doing for centuries.

It was when John turned onto the track to go
back to the Clifftop Cafe to get a cup of tea that it
happened. He was looking for 'Lighthouse' who
was doing his usual search for scraps when John
came across the beach hut that Lynda had owned,
the one that she told John she sold because, "She
didn't need a bolt-hole anymore."

Outside the beach hut, lying peacefully in the
sun, were two dogs tied up, a black Alsatian and a

black giant poodle. John's blood froze. His brain started screaming, "No! no! no!"

He instantly started to sweat. He had to take giant lungfuls of air to stop from passing out. Both dogs looked up, recognised him, and wagged their tales. He forced his legs forward to look through the kitchen window. John's stomach tightened into a million knots. Inside was his brother and his lover, the scene was the same as before. The naked man was on the sofa bed, ankles tied, hands outstretched and handcuffed. The back arched, the head thrown back, the eyes screwed shut in ecstasy. The only view of the woman was the head, covered in black dishevelled hair, going up and down repeatedly between the man's legs.

John turned into an animal as he burst through the door of the beach hut. All the screams that were filling his brain now erupted from his throat as he reached for the kitchen knife. The unnatural sound of a completely insane man brought her head back from the penis. Her look of joyful lust changed to abject horror. With one backhand swipe of the knife, John partially severed Lynda's neck with only the muscles keeping her head in position. Death was instantaneous with jets of blood flooding onto the stomach of the man. Richard looked down in horror and looked up only to take the first half of the kitchen blade fully in the throat. His last plea to John ended in the death rattle.

The water was now up to John's chin. He had to stretch his neck in order to see his final sunset. It was beautiful as usual and just before he drowned, he was able to look to his left to gaze into the lifeless eyes of his lover who he had handcuffed along with his own left hand to the large black iron ring jutting out from the base of the cliff.

He saved his last action to stand completely on his toes to look to his right. He could not see Richard's face as the tide had turned and twisted the body. All John could see was his brother's wrist handcuffed to his own and the end of the knife still protruded from his throat.

The final sunset finished to leave the cliffs of Hunstanton in darkness.

Flying Too Close to the Sun

Chapter One: The First Murder

The first time I raped and murdered a young girl, I have to tell you, it was a complete accident. Well, the murder was anyway. Before you judge me, let me tell you a bit about myself and my background leading up to the incident.

My name is Tommy Lee Jackson. Okay, I know you've heard of me. I know I'm famous. The 'T.L.J.' Radio Show. The breakfast D.J. on 'NOW Radio', the biggest commercial radio station in the U.K. based in London, only a short walk from my million pound apartment across the bridge from the London Eye.

My beautiful wife, Joan, and my gorgeous two year daughter, Poppy, live there. The apartment is the bollocks. Overlooks the Thames and the concierge service is second to none. Every time Joan goes online to do the Tesco shop, when it gets delivered, the concierge not only brings in the delivery but he puts all the groceries away for us. The man's superb. So he should be dealing with punters who can afford to live there.

I digress. You have to understand not only do I get a six figure salary, I'm also known for looking after the advertisers who sponsor my show. If they've got a corporate event, I'm the man to run it for them. If Elton John wants to fly me out to Monte

Carlo for one of his famous fancy dress parties, I'm the D.J. of choice. At five grand a gig, I'm not going to turn that down. I also open new nightclubs, have a regular gig at 'FRESH', London's No 1 nightclub. I've even D.J.'d at children's parties, well it was the Beckhams who requested me. So you see. I'm the man.

So you're saying anyone can play records, anyone can hold a mic. I'm telling you no-one has got my gift. When I arrive at a club gig and go on stage, the atmosphere cranks up tenfold. I connect to the audience. I know exactly what music they want to dance to and I lead the way with top class tracks they haven't even heard yet. I have the gift of giving them a superb night out - guaranteed.

It was at one of these gigs I unintentionally messed up big time.

I was on top form at 'FRESH', my resident Thursday night club gig. Everything was going brilliant with lots of underdressed young women to choose from.

You have to understand, I just love women. Black, white, yellow, they're all the same to me. Now don't get me wrong, I've nothing against lesbians, gays, trannies whatever. All I know is if I was given the choice of sleeping with Naomi Campbell or Graham Norton, it's a no-brainer. You have to understand I am never faithful to my wife. She's at home looking after Poppy and I'm in a different world surrounded by young women who dress like hookers, who want nothing else but to have sex with T.L.J. It gives me a chance to indulge in all kinds of sex - oral, anal, doggy, you name it, I love it. The way I look at it is I make love to my wife and the rest is lust. How does my conscience handle all of this? Well I'm not going to wake my wife up at four in the morning so I might just as well take what's on offer after the gig. I just look upon it as deluxe masterbation.

That night I did the usual. Told my roadie, Ronny, to pick out the best-looking one and, if she wants a lift home with T.L.J., wait for me outside about 100 yards up the road as she must understand I have to be very discreet. Not only do I not want my wife to find out, I also don't want the gutter press to splatter my lifestyle all over their front pages.

I drive off after the gig, spot her 100 yards up the road, stop my Roller and tell to get in the back seat. I know what you're thinking. 'He's got a Rolls Royce!' Well, the way I look at, if Alan Sugar can have one, so can I. In my business not only do you have to be successful, you have to be 'seen' to be successful.

So, getting back to the incident. I drive for a few miles and park up in an isolated area far away from any C.T.V. cameras and I get in the back seat. You're thinking you're going to have sex with a complete stranger? Too right I am. I don't even know her name. I don't want to know their names. When they ask me, when I drop them off home, if I'm going to see them again, I just point at my wedding ring and drive off. At least they've got something to tell their mates at work on Monday morning. "You'll never guess what happened to me Saturday night?" I had sex with T.L.J in the back of his Rolls Royce. He was fantastic."

This particular night, everything was going as normal. I ripped her string thong knickers off as a memento, and I was busy fingering her to get her ready for the famous T.L.J. 8 inch weapon when she started to panic. 'Stop! Stop! I don't want this, I don't want this.' What do you mean 'You don't want this' as I forced my erect penis, full-length, all the way into her very wet vagina. Then the bitch scratched my face. I'd got a 100 quids worth of make-up on for the gig but she still managed to draw blood.

'Stop! Stop! Help! Help! Her screams were getting louder. I'd had enough so I drew my hand back and gave her a right good backhander. That shut her up. I swiftly turned her over and fucked her from behind. I have to tell you when you come and you've already had two lines of Coke and a bottle of Sambuca, it's the business. Talk about mind-blowing. After I finished, I said 'Now you can get out and sod off'. No answer. I turned her over. Her head was at a funny angle. I had broken her neck. Why did I have to hit her so hard? Bloody hell! I didn't mean to kill her - honest.

As I drove home, I formulated a plan on how to get rid of her body. The guy who supplied me and the rest of the top celebrities with any kind of drug had a scrap yard with a vehicle crushing machine in South London. Tomorrow, I would buy an old banger off Ebay, stick her body in the boot, and five grand later, the car will be crushed and put at the back of the yard where it will lay undisturbed for many a year.

I crept into bed at 5:30 in the morning. The wife only grunted and I fell asleep straight away. The next thing I knew, the alarm went off at 7 am. Joan had to get Poppy ready for school and ready herself for work. As she leaned over to kiss me goodbye, the cuff of her uniform caught my eye and I sat up rubbing it.

"Sorry, Love," she said. "See you later. You better get up soon or you'll be late for your beloved listeners." She laughed as she left the room. Now I know what you're thinking. Cuff! Uniform! You're going to love this. My wife is a police constable in the Thames Valley police force.

***

If you stand right at the end of Horseferry Road in London, you're able to see across the River Thames to the MI6 building next to the London Eye. If you turn directly to the right, there is the MI5 building. The anti-tank bollards ten feet apart all around the building is a bit of a give-away to the level of security in the building. Plus there's two armed policemen on patrol all around the building twenty-four seven. These buildings must have cost millions. If you travel back into town along Horseferry Road, you will come to the Channel Four television studios, all stainless steel and glass, a modern structure, once again costing millions.

Halfway between the MI5 and Channel Four buildings is the local station for the Thames Valley Police Force, a building that looks like it had been designed by a five year old with a box of crayons. It was one hundred years old and looking even older. If you go through the large oak doors at the front, you are immediately met with a reception desk with a glass panel incorporating a microphone that the members of the public can speak through.

Joan Jackson had drawn the short straw on this week's rota. Last week, she was on foot patrol in the West End chasing shoplifters and helping to investigate burglaries. This week she's giving directions to Japanese tourists and keeping a look out for Mrs. Jacobs' cat that had a strange habit of walking into the station lured by the smell of Joan's smoked salmon sandwiches. At least it gave Joan time to think. Her daughter, Poppy, was teething so Joan wasn't getting enough sleep and Poppy wasn't her usual keen self when Joan dropped her off at nursery.

Then there was Tommy Lee. Over the last few days, he had been real moody which wasn't like him. He was usually buzzing when he came home from his radio show with stories about who phoned in to discuss the matters of the day and which celebrity did he interview and what was he or she like. Strangely enough, there were no parties for him to go to and he had cancelled his residency at 'FRESH' nightclub, his normal Thursday night gig for a couple of weeks citing 'he was getting a bit stale.'

Joan was dragged out of her reverie when a woman knocked on the glass partition to attract her attention. "My name is Short, Mrs Irene Short. I want to report my daughter missing." As she spoke, she shoved a photograph of a beautiful-looking girl aged about sixteen under the glass partition.

"How long has she been missing for?" asked Joan.

"She hasn't come home for a few nights. That's not unusual but what is unusual is she hasn't phoned and she hasn't answered any of my calls."

"Take a seat and I will ask one of our C.I.D. team to come and take a few details. We only class someone as a missing person if they have been gone for more than forty-eight hours," Joan told the worried-looking Mother.

Just then a young girl came in. "Sorry I'm late Mum, it took ages to get a cab." Joan was confused. The lady sitting down had given her a photograph of the young girl that had just come in. Mrs. Short could see the confused look on Joan's face. "This is Jenny, she's Laura's identical twin sister."

Just then a young detective came through the back door of reception, lifted the hatch, and whilst shaking Mrs. Short's hand, introduced himself. "Hi, my name is Detective Constable Tony Johnson." He showed Mrs. Short his warrant card to prove his identity.

"My name is Irene Short and this is my daughter, Jenny, whose twin sister, Laura, has gone missing from a night out at 'FRESH' nightclub last Thursday evening."

"If you'd like to come through to my office, I can take the details and we can get the investigation underway."

"I'm coming as well," said Jenny.

"I want her to come as well." Jenny was pointing at Joan.

"I'm sorry, Miss, Police Constable Jackson is not on the C.I.D. team."

Jenny turned to her mum and pleaded "Mum, you have to bring this policewoman into the interview room as well. I can feel it, Mum."

"Feel what?" asked Tony.

"I'm her identical twin sister and I can feel that this police woman knows something about why Laura has gone missing."

"How could she know anything?" asked Tony.

"She just does," replied Jenny. "Mum, you've got to tell them when Laura and I have our feelings about each other, we are always right." Jenny's Mum nodded. Jenny turned to Joan, pointed directly at her and said "You know what happened to Laura, I can feel it."

***

"You'll never guess what happened at work today?" said Joan to a rather disinterested Tommy Lee.

"What?" he replied, not looking up from his newspaper.

"A lady came into the station today and reported her daughter missing."

"She's most likely at some all-night party," suggested Tommy Lee.

"No," replied Joan, "she's been missing since last Thursday." Tommy Lee's ears pricked up. "The funny thing about it is her twin sister maintains she can feel things and she more or less accused me of knowing where the girl was. How mad is that?"

How mad indeed, thought Tommy Lee, his stomach muscles tightening. "Well, I've got some news for you as well."

"What's that?" asked Joan.

"The radio station wants me to broadcast my show from Las Vegas next week to cover the Oscars presentations."

"That's brilliant," replied Joan, giving Tommy Lee a big hug. "How long will you be away for?" asked Joan.

"About a week" replied Tommy Lee.

***

While Joan is away picking Poppy up from her Mum's, I might as well come clean with you lot. The station didn't ask me to go to Las Vegas, I practically begged them to let me go. I was called into the controller, Dick James', office. He more or less sacked me on the spot.

"What's wrong with you, T.J.? Your ratings have plummeted. Your interviewing technique is boring. Our advertisers and our shareholders want to know what's going on. Are you ill or something?"

"I just need a break. I've been burning the candle from both ends, taking too many private gigs, not putting the show first. I promise it'll all change. Put me on that Las Vegas gig and I'll bring the old Tommy Lee back with me."

"I've promised that gig to Tammy Knight, our new female jock. It's the new trend T.J. Woman D.J.'s are taking over," said Dick.

"Please, Boss, give me the gig. Something new to get my teeth into. A few days away, some great shows broadcast from Las Vegas and I'll come back a new man."

Dick replied, "Okay, T.J., this is your last chance. If things don't improve when you come back from Las Vegas, I'm going to replace you with Tammy, got that?"

So you see, yours truly is skating on thin ice.

***

The front door opened and an excited Poppy ran into the arms of her dad. "Hello sweet cheeks, are you going to be a good girl while your daddy is

away? If so, Daddy will bring you back a present."
Poppies eyes widened and she gave her daddy
another hug.

It was then that Joan gave Tommy Lee some
devastating news. "You'll never guess, Tommy,
what happened today."

"Guess what?" replied T.J.

"I've been put on the investigating team for
Laura's disappearance. They want me to be with
them all the time."

"What do you mean?" asked Tommy.

"I'm going to be their Family Liaison officer."

Chapter Two. The Second Murder

If you've ever seen an advert for Las Vegas, they always use the front shot of the Bellagio Hotel with its fabulous fountain show leaping into the Nevada skyline. The two towers offer nearly four thousand rooms over thirty-six floors. Who'd want to be a cleaner, eh! You just cannot imagine it! A decent room will set you back two hundred dollars and if you want to use the gym at any time, it's a further eighty dollars.

Tommy Lee was impressed with his trip to the Oscars presentation night at the Bellagio. His non-stop flight from Heathrow was first class and it was the first time he turned left going into an aeroplane instead of usually turning right into the cheap seats.

After a couple of complimentary glasses of champagne, he pressed the lever that turned his seat into a full-length bed and slept most of the way.

He was met at the airport by the radio producer, just call me Sandy, who was going to help Tommy Lee gain admission not only to the presentation night itself, but to the all-important after show parties where all the 'A' listers would attend to get those paparazzi photographs that would be in the world's newspapers the following day. Tommy Lee was hoping he would be regarded as an essential interviewer to maintain their profile to all of his listeners in the U.K.

Sandy had hired a brand new Mercedes for Tommy Lee to use during his time off, although he did point out, apart from Las Vegas itself, there was nothing but desert all around if he felt the need to go sightseeing.

***

The producer was obviously gay, which didn't bother Tommy Lee, as quite a high percentage of guys involved in the movie business were gay. If it helped open a few more doors, Tommy Lee was up for anything.

The presentation night was fabulous. Las Vegas is the centre of America's show business and The Bellagio pulled out all of the stops to ensure the visiting paparazzi were looked after. There was a welcome gift pack on his bed that contained not only the new iPad but also the new Apple Watch. It was rumoured the top stars' Apple gifts were solid gold.

Tommy Lee ensured he was a bit above the celebrity ladder when he told a little white lie and said 'NOW Radio' was the biggest radio station in the U.K. He had missed out the word 'commercial'. Tommy Lee was quick to notice that no one from Radio 1 or even Radio 2 was present at the awards ceremony so he saw it as an opportunity to 'big up' the listener figures of 'NOW Radio' when he got back to the hotel and had his initial meeting with Sandy.

Sandy suggested that instead of broadcasting his show from Sandy's radio station, Las Vegas Radio International, Sandy would use the first night's programme to interview Tommy Lee so that Sandy's listeners would get to know Tommy Lee. The time of Sandy's radio show was ideal as Sandy was the 'drive time' D.J. for L.V.R.I. His show went out at 5pm every afternoon Monday to Friday which suited Tommy Lee's usual breakfast listeners as, with the eight hour time difference, the show would be broadcasted at 9am in the U.K.

Tommy Lee was determined to stay off the drugs and the booze. He knew his career was in jeopardy so, without the intoxicants, he knew he could remain sharp whilst on air.

The first evening show went well. Tommy Lee was funny, interesting and handled the phone-ins from Sandy's American listeners with ease. When Sandy handed over to the night time D.J., he took off his headphones, shook hands with Tommy Lee and congratulated him on a great show.

"Now it's time to go to the presentation of this year's Oscars. Be prepared for a long night as it's not just the main presentation we have to sit through. Obviously, 'The Joker' and 'Judy' are favourites in all four of their nominations but we have to sit through the Oscars for the best animation picture, best director for the best foreign film, best short feature and so on. By the time we get to the first party, and it's always Elton John's, it will be getting onto well after midnight. I've managed to get us into three parties in total. I will come with you holding a handheld camera. You get a better response when they think they are being filmed, with you holding your microphone."

Tommy Lee was really looking forward to getting some great material from a lot of major stars so it was with a high level of excitement when he sat in the back with Sandy of the stretch limousine that had been hired just for the special occasion. Tommy Lee was wearing a really smart white dinner jacket with a black shirt and white dicky bow. He wanted to stand out as all the other guys in their 'penguin' suits looked as though they were off to play in a snooker tournament.

It only took ten minutes to travel from the radio station to the Bellagio so the stretch limousine seemed a bit over the top. That was until they arrived and there were stretch limos queuing up around the water fountain features. There was little reaction when they were dropped off as everyone was clambering for Tom Cruise's autograph.

Tommy Lee was a little disappointed when they were guided by a hotel personality girl to their seats which were at the back of the room. Tommy Lee craned his neck to see if he could recognise the 'A' listers sitting at the front. They were all there, even actors and actresses who weren't nominated.

The Oscars was definitely the night to be seen at. Sandy had been correct about the length of time it took. After the initial start of 5pm, it was after midnight when the final Oscar was awarded.

The after Oscars parties couldn't have gone better. First of all, he was able to grab Elton John for a few words of congratulations about winning the Oscars for 'best original song' alongside Bernie Taupin with the song from the 'Rocket Man' movie 'I'm Gonna Love Me Again.' TJ was able to keep Elton's interest for a few more minutes by discussing the prospects of Watford Town F.C. who were currently languishing at the bottom of the Premier League. Elton had always supported Watford and was Chairman of the club for a while. All good stuff for Tommy Lee's listeners.

Tommy Lee managed interviews with the four stars of 'The Irishman' - Joe Pesci, Robert De Nero, Al Pacino and Harvey Keitel. He was pleased that he had watched the movie on the aeroplane and was prepared for asking the relevant questions such as the fact it was the first time all four major movie stars had worked together.

It was impossible to interview Joaquin Phoenix and Renee Zellweger, both winners of best actor and best actress, as there was a scrum of paparazzi surrounding them but he did manage to get a few valuable minutes with Brad Pitt, winner of best supporting actor.

By the time he made it to the third after show party, he had more than enough material to fill the three scheduled shows he was to broadcast before he returned to England. His interview with George McKay, star of '1917', didn't go down too well as it was obvious that the champagne had already kicking in and everybody just wanted to party.

Tommy Lee was about to leave, sober as a judge, and after saying 'goodnight' to Sandy, he was approached by an absolutely stunning blonde. "Hi, are you one of the nominees?"

"No! I wish," replied Tommy Lee, laughing at the thought, "I'm a radio D.J. sent from England to get some interviews for my show which I'm broadcasting here in Las Vegas for the next three drive time shows for L.V.I.R."

"Did you manage to get some good material?"

All in all, they must have talked for over an hour. Cindy, an aspiring actress, was networking and trying to get some valuable contacts, hoping to secure some auditions for future movies. She was curious to find out what the big movie stars were really like and Tommy Lee was only too pleased to tell her. He hadn't touched a drop of drink all night but thought "sod it," he'd done a great nights work and one or two drinks wasn't going to hurt. As you know, one drink is too many and ten drinks are not enough.

A couple of hours later, Tommy Lee found himself back in his hotel room after inviting Cindy in for a night cap, and he was feeling on top of the world. He had enough material for three brilliant shows and here he was, convinced he was about to have sex with a gorgeous blonde.

As Tommy Lee handed Cindy a rather large brandy, she searched in her handbag for something.

"I suppose we'd better get the 'business' end of the transaction out of the way before we settle down for the night."

"Settle down for the night? Transaction? What are you talking about?"

Cindy found what she was looking for in her handbag and whilst passing a credit card machine to Tommy Lee, stated, "It's a thousand dollars for straight sex, another five hundred if you want me to stay the night."

Tommy was gobsmacked. "You're a hooker?" he exclaimed.

"Well, you don't think I could afford to live in Las Vegas serving drinks at the local Hooters bar, do you? Oh, and by the way, I don't take American Express."

Tommy could feel that old familiar sensation of an inner rage about to explode. Perhaps if he hadn't drunk so much, things could have worked out differently. "Sod that! there's no way I'm paying for sex. I never have and don't intend to start now."

It turned out to be quite ironic. Here was a guy with no ethics and no scruples whatsoever trying to claim he had certain standards to live up to.

***

Tommy made an attempt to grab Cindy and escort her from the room when she grabbed the portable credit card machine and smashed it into his face. Tommy went down on one knee dazed, and tasting the blood coming from his bottom lip.

"You're going to regret that, you bitch."

Tommy had his right arm behind him as he got ready to hit Cindy but halfway through standing up, he stopped as he was now looking down the barrel of a snub-nosed Saturday Night Special pistol, a small gun, designed to fit into a lady's handbag, but lethal if fired from a short distance.

"Give me your wallet. I'm not working tonight for nothing." Cindy's eyes were pure evil and Tommy Lee was in no doubt the gun would be fired if he didn't do what he was told to do.

As he put his hand inside his jacket pocket, he deliberately dropped his wallet on the floor. Then, while he was bending down to pick it up, he grabbed Cindy's wrist and tried to wrestle the gun from her. During the struggle, they both fell. At the same time, there was the sound of Cindy's wrist cracking and the muffled sound of the pistol firing a nine millimetre bullet directly into Cindy's heart. Cindy's body went limp and Tommy Lee struggled to his feet.

"What the hell do I do now?" He felt for her pulse but she was clearly dead.

Tommy Lee momentarily thought about going to the police and trying to explain what happened. After all, it was a complete accident. He decided against it as he would be arrested and, giving his strained relationship with his boss, he would most likely be fired if the police held him in custody thus not allowing Tommy Lee to do his radio shows.

There was, surprisingly, very little blood from the small hole in Cindy's heart. Tommy Lee picked up the body and walked it to the hotel lift which was, luckily, adjacent to his room. He took the lift down to the basement where the hotel car park was and managed to put the body into the boot of the Mercedes without anybody seeing him. The only thing he could think of was to drive as far away as possible into the desert where he could bury the body. He knew it was a four hour drive westwards to Los Angeles so he decided to drive for a couple of hours and then, hopefully, find an exit off the highway to allow him to drive into the desert.

It was a clear moonlight night so he was able to drive, after turning off the highway, for about half an hour into the desert where he spent a good hour finding suitable rocks which would cover the body completely. Satisfied that, hopefully, the body wouldn't be spotted by vultures or any other wildlife, Tommy Lee headed back to his hotel.

He called room service as soon as he got back to have his clothes dry cleaned and then went straight to bed to try and get some sleep. All he could think of was the sound of the gun going off. It was a lot quieter than he expected perhaps because the barrel was pressed tightly against Cindy's heart. There was no response from anyone in the hotel so, thank God, he had gotten away with that side of things. All he needed now was the body to lay undiscovered so he could be back in England free and clear.

It was no use, he couldn't sleep.

Unfortunately over the next three days, the radio shows were a joke. Sandy kept asking him what was wrong. Tommy Lee said he thought he may have caught a virus. The bright, breezy, funny, articulate disc jockey of old had long disappeared and Tommy Lee knew that when he went back to England he would be fired. He had that one chance to get back on track and a damn hooker had blown it all for him. Not for a minute did Tommy Lee feel sorry for what had happened. Cindy had drawn the gun and had paid the consequences. In a life filled with drink and drugs with everyone bowing to your every wish, Tommy Lee loved the celebrity side of his life. He couldn't imagine a life without it all. He thought that no matter what he did, it was someone else's fault.

Tommy Lee phoned home regularly at the U.K.'s tea time, more to speak to Poppy than his wife. On his last day in Las Vegas, Joan gave him some terrible news. The only bit of C.C.T.V. the police had unearthed from Laura Short's last movements was her talking and laughing at length with the D.J., Tommy Lee Jackson, and the police want to interview Tommy Lee as soon as he came back to the U.K.

Tommy Lee could hardly string two words together on his last show. It was a good job he had enough material interviewing a lot of major movie

245

stars so he filled the three hour slot with all the interviews and kept his own input to a minimum.

He tried to get some sleep on the way back to England on the aeroplane. He thought having a few brandies would help but, unfortunately, several episodes of turbulence didn't help, and he arrived in Heathrow absolutely knackered.

The police were waiting for him at arrivals and took him straight to Horse Ferry Road police station. Detective Constable Tony Johnson was waiting for him and showed him footage from the club's C.C.T.V. cameras. He had passed his wife, Joan, who was manning the reception, but wasn't allowed to speak to her.

"Mister Jackson, can we have your thoughts about this footage of you talking and laughing with Laura Short only hours before she went missing?"

Tommy Lee had anticipated that the police had probably already spoken to his roadie, Ronny, and had his answers well-prepared.

"Officer, I can't really say I remember the girl as there are many who come up and ask for requests to play their favourite records or give a 'shout out' to one of their mates who may be on a hen night. My job is a lot more than just playing music. My responsibility is to liaise with the club security in case of any trouble. I'm in the best position to spot any trouble brewing so that is my main duty as well as controlling the atmosphere through whatever mix of music I decide to play. I know what you're about to bring up. What about my roadie, Ronny, looking out for the best-looking girls who might want a lift home? This girl, what's her name? Laura! She may have been the chosen one that night but I can assure you, and if you check the outside C.C.T.V. cameras, you'll see that I drove away from the club that night with just me in my car, no passengers whatsoever."

"The chosen one? A strange choice of words," said the detective. 'So having one night stands with young girls is a regular occurrence for you, is it?"

"I'm assuming it's not my lifestyle you are investigating officer. The main point is you can clearly see I left the club alone that night and went straight home."

"Your wife is unable to confirm the time as she was asleep."

"I'm not in the habit of waking her up when I come in from work."

Tommy Lee was allowed to leave with strict instructions not to leave the country as the police may want to interview him at a later date.

You could cut the atmosphere with a knife when Tommy Lee got home. His wife kept asking him about Laura Short. He was the last person to see Laura alive. What was this about your roadie picking out young girls for you?! Why does Jenny Short keep going on about Joan and insists she knows what happened to her sister?

Tommy Lee ended up slamming the door and went to bed for a much-needed sleep.

***

247

He delayed the inevitable at the radio station by calling in sick the next morning. He claimed he picked up a virus in Las Vegas and he had been to his doctor who had taken some blood to see if he could find out what was wrong with him.

After Joan left for work, taking Poppy with her to drop her off at nursery, things got worse for a despondent Tommy Lee. The shrill sound of his ringtone jolted Tommy Lee out of his mood.

"Hello, Tommy Lee Jackson speaking."

"My name is Officer Jack Griffiths calling on behalf of the Las Vegas Police Department. I have been investigating a missing person's case about a young lady who was seen speaking to you at the Belvoir Hotel and I was hoping you could help me."

"How did you get my mobile number?"

"With the help of the Bellagio Hotel, I was able to get the telephone number of the radio station that you work who gave me your contact details. I understand you're off work with a virus today?"

"Yes, it must be something I picked up on the flight back to the U.K."

"Well, Mister Jackson, the missing person is Miss Cindy Starr, which is her stage name, and she is really Belinda O'Brien, a mother of two girls. She is, or was, a well-known 'lady of the night' with two convictions of grievous body harm. She gets nasty when she does not get paid apparently."

"What's this got to do with me?" asked Tommy.

"When we were notified that you were the last person to speak to her, we were able to do a forensic search of your hotel room and we found traces of Belinda's blood on the carpet."

"How do you know she wasn't in the room previously?"

"I need for you to go to your local police station at Queensberry Road. They're aware that you will be coming in, and let them take a blood sample so we can eliminate you from our inquiries. Are you prepared to do that for us, sir?"

"Certainly officer, I'll get onto it straight away."

"Many thanks, Mister Jackson." With that, Tommy Lee's phone went dead.

***

When Joan came home from work, he lied through his teeth. "I have to go your police station to get a blood test. There was some trouble at the Bellagio Hotel in Las Vegas and the police need to eliminate me from their enquiries."

"That's good," replied Joan." D.I. Johnson, if you remember, is heading up the investigation into Laura Short's disappearance. He wants to interview you further. They've found additional C.C.T.V. footage showing clearly there was someone in the back of your car."

Tommy Lee was feeling the noose tighten further around his neck.

"Please can you just tell me the truth? You know I will stand by you no matter what happens. The girl's parents and family are going out of their minds."

Yeah, stand by me? No chance, thought Tommy Lee. What was he going to do?

He was sitting in front of the T.V. an hour later not really watching it when Joan entered the room with a suitcase and Polly all wrapped up in her outside clothes. "I think it may be best if I stay at my mother's until this has settled down. Laura's twin sister started kicking off today when the police showed your Rolls Royce to the Short family. They are going to televise a reconstruction tomorrow using C.C.T.V. footage clearly showing your car. It'll be in all the papers. I can't handle the thought of the paparazzi camping on our front door."

Tommy Lee never looked up as his wife and beloved daughter left the room. He knew he was finished.

***

"Well folks, this will be our last conversation together. As usual, I am recording everything on my smart phone for posterity so the police can solve the case of Laura Short. I'm assuming the Las Vegas police will let you know about the death of Cindy Star as well. I have driven down to Beachy Head, a notorious suicide spot near Eastbourne. I reckon with a good five hundred yard run-up, the Roller could be going over 100 mph before we crash, nose first, on the rocks over three hundred feet below. I've come here tonight because I don't know what else to do."

He took a deep intake of breath before continuing, "Classed as a pedophile by all and sundry, my life in a prison will be hell. I'm just going to be a statistic to the other 500 poor souls who have come to Beach Head to provide the final answer. I'll leave my phone in my rucksack in clear view for the police to find it and, obviously, it will reveal all. As well as the American incident, I have revealed the whereabouts of Laura's body. I cannot get my head around how callous I was getting rid of her body like I was sweeping some dust underneath a carpet. So goodbye to everyone who knew me. My apologies to my wife Joan and the horrors she will have to live through and, most of all, my all-consuming love for my little girl, Poppy. She is the only human being I have never lied to. Please give her a final kiss from her daddy."

***

Tommy Lee Jackson was wrong about the 100mph prediction. Because of wet grass leading up to the white cliffs, the £200k. Rolls Royce had only managed 60mph. It was enough for it to fly like a swan as it arced gracefully down to the rocks below, with twelve air bags exploding simultaneously on impact. It was enough to save Tommy Lee's life. As he lay crushed against the steering wheel, he had just enough time to give one more of those famous last grins reserved exclusively for his audience.

He smelt the strong whiff of petrol vapour and heard the roar of the petrol fire starting against the four red hot exhaust pipes. His life went up in flames as a series of explosions from the twin fuel tanks tore the car apart.

His last thought was *this is what happens when you fly too close to the sun.*